Fargo turned and saw a branch being brushed back just as the near-naked figure dived at him, tomahawk in hand. Only Fargo's superb reflexes let him pull his head to the side in time to avoid the edge of the tomahawk as it plunged downward, scraping his ear and slamming into the ground.

The Indian pulled the short-handled axe free to strike again, but Fargo brought his knee up and sank it into the man's groin. The Indian let out a grunt of pain as he fell back for a moment, giving enough time for Fargo to swing a short, hard left hook. It caught the man alongside the head and he fell sideways. Fargo rolled and leaped up to charge, but had to dive away as his attacker brought the tomahawk around in a short, vicious arc. . . .

THE TRAILSMAN
#212

SIOUX STAMPEDE

by

Jon Sharpe

A SIGNET BOOK

SIGNET
Published by New American Library, a division of
Penguin Putnam Inc., 375 Hudson Street,
New York, New York 10014, U.S.A.
Penguin Books Ltd, 27 Wrights Lane,
London W8 5TZ, England
Penguin Books Australia Ltd,
Ringwood, Victoria, Australia
Penguin Books Canada Ltd, 10 Alcorn Avenue,
Toronto, Ontario, Canada M4V 3B2
Penguin Books (N.Z.) Ltd, 182–190 Wairau Road,
Auckland 10, New Zealand

Penguin Books Ltd, Registered Offices:
Harmondsworth, Middlesex, England

Published by Signet, an imprint of New American Library, a division of
Penguin Putnam, Inc.

First Printing, July 1999
10 9 8 7 6 5 4 3 2 1

The first chapter of this book originally appeared in *Badlands Bloodbath*,
the two hundred eleventh volume in this series.

 REGISTERED TRADEMARK—MARCA REGISTRADA

Printed in the United States of America

The Trailsman

Beginnings . . . they bend the tree and they mark the man. Skye Fargo was born when he was eighteen. Terror was his midwife, vengeance his first cry. Killing spawned Skye Fargo, ruthless, cold-blooded murder. Out of the acrid smoke of gunpowder still hanging in the air, he rose, cried out a promise never forgotten.

The Trailsman they began to call him all across the West: searcher, scout, hunter, the man who could see where others only looked, his skills for hire but not his soul, the man who lived each day to the fullest, yet trailed each tomorrow. Skye Fargo, the Trailsman, and the seeker who could take the wildness of a land and the wanting of a woman and make them his own.

*1860, Minnesota, north of the
Red Lake country, where old hatreds
rose to bring new death and the
only answer was to do the
wrong thing for the right reason. . . .*

Fargo groaned. The pounding that seemed like it was about to split his head open grew worse. Lying naked, the sheet barely covering his groin, he rose up on one elbow, his eyes blinking harshly as they scanned the little room, past the large porcelain pitcher of water on the battered dresser and the faded floral hotel wallpaper. Through dry lips, he managed a blasphemous oath. The pounding was not just in his head, it seemed. Some of it was coming from the door, adding insult to injury, elevating the throbbing in his temples to new heights. Rising on one elbow, he managed to find his voice as he peered at the door.

"It's open, dammit," he rasped.

The door flew open and a figure stormed into the room. The first thing Fargo saw was carrot red hair cut short, then a tall form clothed in a white blouse and a denim skirt. He squinted at a face that might have been pretty if it weren't wreathed in frowns and drawn tight in anger. He saw her eyes move across the muscled nakedness of his body, stopping momentarily at his groin, then returning to his face. "You're drunk," she bit out. "Stinking, rotten drunk." She spit the words out with a combination of shock and fury.

"Wrong," he said, his mouth feeling full of cotton. "I was drunk. And I expect to get drunk again. But I'm not right now."

"This room smells like a bourbon still," she snapped. "You're shameful, useless."

"If you say so, honey," he muttered, falling back on the bed and putting one arm over his eyes. "Now, get the hell out of here."

"I'll do nothing of the sort," Fargo heard her say.

He winced silently under his arm. "Sister, you're in the wrong place at the wrong time for the wrong reasons. Now, take off," he said.

"You're Skye Fargo, aren't you?" he heard her question.

"Last time I looked," he muttered, groaning at the now severe pounding in his head.

"Then I'm not in the wrong place. But you're a terrible disappointment," the young woman said.

Fargo took his arm away from his face and peered at her. Only her flaming red hair came to his bleary eyes clearly. "Get out, honey, whoever you are," he muttered. "Now, dammit."

"No, I'm staying right here. You're going to sober up and keep your word," she snapped.

He screwed his face up at her. "Keep my word about what?" he asked.

"You know what," she answered.

"Honey, I don't know what the hell you're talking about but I know I want you out of here," Fargo said.

2

"No," she threw back defiantly.

He lifted his head and winced at the pain it caused. "You ever been thrown out of a hotel room by a very angry, naked man, honey?" he asked and squinted at her.

"I've never been thrown out of a hotel room by anyone, naked or dressed," she returned indignantly.

"There's a first time for everything. You've got ten seconds to get your ass out of here on your own," Fargo said, then he fell back on the bed, closed his eyes, and cursed the incessant pounding in his brain.

"You're not getting away with this," she said threateningly and he heard her spin and start to stride away. His eyes were still closed when the pitcher of ice water hit him full in the face.

"Crap!" he roared as he shuddered, and started to wrench his eyes open when the pitcher itself followed, smashing into his head. "Goddamn," he swore as new pain shot through his skull, and he felt the room spinning. He shook his head to clear it and swung his long legs from the bed. The room was still spinning, and he sat quietly for a moment as he heard the door slam shut. Shaking his head again, he pushed to his feet. "Goddamn these women," he yelled at the closed door. He muttered further curses at all redheaded females when his eyes fell upon the straight-backed chair where he'd hung his clothes. Only his clothes were no longer there, everything gone now except his boots.

Letting out an exasperated sigh, he strode for the door and stopped when he realized he was buck naked. Turning, he pulled the sheet from the bed and wrapped it around himself like a·Roman toga. He then took down his gunbelt, still hanging from the bedpost where he'd put it the night before, and strapped it around his waist to hold the sheet in place. Pulling on his boots, Fargo strode from the room, seeing the hallway outside was empty. Sun streaming through a hall window told him it was well into morning, and he proceeded past the front desk. The clerk, an older man in pince-nez spectacles, looked up at him. "Where'd she go?" Fargo barked.

"Out," the clerk replied. "In a hurry."

Fargo left the town's only inn, The Equity Hotel, squinting as the bright sunlight assaulted him. But anger had now pushed aside some of the throbbing in his head as he halted at a man standing by the hitching post. "Girl just left here," Fargo began, seeing the man's eyes move questioningly up and down the sheet tied around him. "Don't say it," Fargo growled. "You see her?"

"Carrot top?" the man asked.

"That's her," Fargo said.

"Rode north out of town, hell-bent for leather," the man said.

"What was she riding?" Fargo pressed.

"Big Cleveland bay, dappled hindquarters. Couldn't help noticing him. Don't see many."

"Much obliged," Fargo said and the man let his eyes move over the sheet again.

"Must've been some night," he commented gaily.

Fargo threw a harsh glare at him as he hurried down

the street, ignoring the stares and hoots that followed him from the cowhands he passed. He found the general store and stepped inside. The storekeepers's eyes widened at once. "No smart-ass talk, mister," Fargo warned and silently cursed the ludicrousness of his appearance. "I want drawers, jeans, and a shirt. Everything large and hurry up."

"Yes, sir," the storekeeper said smartly, then stepped to a rack at the rear of the store and returned in moments, putting the clothes on the counter. His hand went out to rest on the apparel as Fargo reached for them. "How do you figure to pay for these, mister?" the merchant asked.

"I'll be paying for them when I get back," Fargo said.

"You got any way to prove that, stranger?" the storekeeper said.

Fargo drew his Colt. "Here's proof for now. I don't have time to argue. You'll be paid, my word on it. Now stand back, dammit," he snarled. Obeying the angry blue ice of the big man's eyes, the storekeep stepped back and watched as Fargo tossed aside the sheet and pulled on clothes that seemed to fit well enough. "I'll be back, believe me," Fargo said as he strode from the store and ran to the town stable where he'd put his horse. He saddled up the Ovaro and tossed the stableboy his saddle pouch, worth three times the stable fee. "It's yours till I get back," he said. Outside, the sun revealed the Ovaro's beauty, setting his jet black fore-and-hindquarters glistening, his pure white midsection gleaming.

Fargo sent the pinto north out of town as his eyes searched the hoofprints that crowded each other in the dry soil. He had ridden about a quarter of a mile beyond town when he was able to isolate the hoofprints he sought, the Cleveland bay's prints being wider and longer than those of most horses. He saw the prints go on for another fifty yards, then turn from the road, traveling along terrain between rows of red ash. A frown dug into Fargo's brow. There were other prints following the Cleveland bay's wide hoofmarks. They had swung in behind when the bay left the road, three sets, he noted, staying close together. The frown still creased his brow as he sent the Ovaro into a fast canter. The three sets of hoofprints stayed together, definitely following the bay as they turned suddenly between a row of thick-trunked, ancient red ash giants.

Fargo caught sight of a small pond sparkling in the sun directly ahead when he heard the short scream, a voice he remembered very well. "Let go of me!" he heard, followed by a sharp gasp of pain. Fargo pulled the pinto to a halt and swung from the saddle. Dropping into a crouch, he silently ran forward, seeing the figures take shape in a small clearing by the pond. Once more, the carrot red crop of hair caught his eye before anything else. Three men came into sight, one holding the young woman, pinning her arms behind her. He noted their three horses together, the Cleveland bay beside a flat rock at the edge of the pond. Fargo crept to the edge of the trees, dropping to one knee. The man holding the young woman had a pudgy-cheeked, baby face that didn't seem to match the thin cruelty of his lips.

"Damn you," the woman said and brought her shoe down hard on the man's ankle. He roared in pain, his grip loosening, allowing the young woman to pull away. She turned to run when one of the others brought her to the ground with a flying tackle. He held her down as the baby-faced one rose and hit her across the face with the back of his hand.

"Goddamn little bitch," he swore and yanked her to her feet as the other one kept hold of her arms. The third man, a thin, sharp-nosed figure with stringy black hair, stepped forward.

"Real little piece of dynamite, isn't she?" he cackled lecherously.

"Yeah. She'll shore be fun to screw," the baby-faced one said.

"Me first," the angular one cut in.

"Why you?" the third man asked.

"I'm the one whose idea it was to follow her to town," the sharp-nosed one said.

"What about getting rid of her?" the third man asked.

"No reason we can't enjoy ourselves, first," the pudgy-cheeked one replied, reaching out and grabbing the girl's calves, pulling her legs out from under her as she went down. The third man kept her arms pinned tightly behind her. "You can go next," he growled and fell to his knees, looming over the girl.

"Rotten, stinking bastards!" the young woman bit

out, turning and twisting her torso as she kicked out with both legs.

"Hold her still, dammit," the baby-faced one snapped as he lowered himself over the young woman, and began to push her skirt up. Fargo drew the big Colt. Putting a bullet into the one half atop her would be easy enough, but his finger stayed poised against the trigger. Sure, it would be easy, but still very risky. The bullet from the powerful Colt could go right through him and into the young woman beneath him. Fargo grimaced, rose to his feet, and stepped into the open.

"That'll be all, mister," he growled, seeing the three men freeze in place for a moment. The sharp-nosed one turned first, spinning to face the voice and starting to reach for his gun. "Wouldn't try that," Fargo said calmly. The man eyed the Colt leveled at him, then let his hand drop to his side. But his eyes told Fargo he was waiting for a better moment. "Get off her," Fargo said to the baby-faced one still leaning over the girl. The man pushed himself up, and thought about going for his gun when he saw the Colt shift a fraction of an inch to point at his chest.

"Who the hell are you?" he blurted.

"That's no matter to you," Fargo said.

"You know her?" the man asked.

"In a way," Fargo said, his eyes flicking to the young woman, seeing the mixture of hope and fear on her face as the third man still held on to her.

"You've got two seconds to get out of here alive," the baby-faced one said.

"Can't do that," Fargo replied evenly.

Pudgy cheeks lifted his head in disbelief. "You some kind of crazy? You figure to take on all three of us?" the man said.

Fargo smiled. "Like sitting ducks," he said. "You boys have only one thing to decide: who gets shot first." He saw the three exchange quick, uneasy glances, keeping the calm smile on his lips. Fargo had already won the first round. He'd made them suddenly unsure of themselves, uncertain of the man they faced. If they drew on him, they'd do so nervously, jerkiness replacing smooth motion. He knew he could outdraw any one of them, but still he'd added precious split seconds to his advantage. They continued to hesitate, and Fargo noted the baby-faced man's fingers twitching. "You want to let her go now?" Fargo said quietly. "I'm a man with a short fuse."

"You're a man with a short life," the sharp-nosed one threw back, but there was only nervous bravado in his voice.

"Your call," Fargo said, shifting the Colt for emphasis, when the third one still holding on to the girl proved he was the smartest of the trio.

"Pull that trigger and she gets it," he called. Fargo flicked his glance at him and cursed silently. The man had drawn his gun, and now had it pushed into the young woman's ribs. In a flash, everything had changed, Fargo realized. His advantage had vanished. It had all become a new and deadly game. But he knew one thing. He had to play it out. He couldn't let them think they had seized the upper hand or the carrot-topped woman was finished. He let his eyes bore into the man holding her, lifting his shoulders in a shrug.

"You do your thing. I'll do mine," Fargo said and saw surprise come into the man's eyes.

"Thought she was a friend of yours," the man said.

"Not exactly," Fargo said.

"Then what the hell are you doin' here?" the baby-faced one broke in.

"She has something of mine I want back. I don't much care if she's dead or alive so long as I get it," Fargo said steadily as he drew the hammer back on the Colt. "You can get yourselves killed with her or not." He waited as his stomach churned. Fargo was playing the bluff to the end, and he was afraid one of them would do the wrong thing and the standoff would burst out of control. And it was the girl who would pay the price. He grew more certain that that was going to happen with every passing second. The one with the gun in her ribs had become the key player, the most dangerous of all of them, now. His head and shoulders were in the open behind the redhead, whose eyes now showed only fear and desperation.

Fargo drew a deep breath. He knew only someone with his marksmanship, and the accuracy of a Colt, had a chance at making the shot. But he had no choice. He couldn't take the two in front of him, first. It would trigger the man holding the girl into firing, and that was the first thing he was trying to prevent. Fargo glanced at the man, drawing a mental bead on his target, allowing himself another split second before pressing the trigger. He had time only to see the man's skull explode in a shower of red and hear the girl scream, and then he was diving, catapulting himself to the ground and rolling away from where he stood.

He heard the volley of shots from the other two as they drew and fired, feeling some of the bullets whizzing past him. But, as he had expected, they fired too quickly and unevenly. Fargo was now in the trees, rolling onto his stomach on a bed of lance-shaped smartweed as he saw the sharp-nosed man turn to fire at the girl. The Colt barked out two shots that almost blended together as one, and the man staggered, spun, and collapsed. Fargo's lake blue eyes turned away, seeking out the third man, and found the baby-faced figure had already reached the horses. "Hold it right there and you can see tomorrow," Fargo called. The man paused, one hand on the saddle horn of his horse, then turned to fire a volley of shots into the trees where Fargo's voice had echoed. Two of the bullets dug into the ground inches from his elbow as he steadied the Colt.

The man had swung onto his horse when Fargo fired. The horse rose up, its forefeet flailing the air as its rider fell backward over its rump. The man hit the ground and lay still. "Damned fool," Fargo muttered, holstering the Colt as he rose, then stepped from the trees and walked toward the young woman as she pushed to her feet. Her dark azure eyes leveled at him as he reached her, her lips parted, her words coated with awe. "It all happened so fast," she stammered.

"That's usually the way," Fargo said.

Her eyes continued to peer hard at him. "Thank you," she managed to say.

He grunted in reply. "Wait here," he said and went to where the baby-faced man lay beside the horses. He knelt down, went through the man's pockets, and found nothing to identify him. His saddlebag held nothing either, and Fargo quickly checked the other two with the same results. But he found himself frowning as a strange odor sifted into his nostrils. Turning, he followed his nose, finding the aroma leading to the horses. The odor grew stronger, much of it coming from their hooves, pasterns, and ankles. *Must have been something they had walked in*, he thought, frowning, and drew the odor into his nostrils again. It was a dark smell, dank and slightly moldy, with a sharp pungency to it. He'd smelled it before, he reckoned, not often, but enough to remember. But he still couldn't put a name to it. Setting it aside in his mind, he returned to where the young woman waited and had the first opportunity to really look at her without bourbon or sixguns in his way.

The carrot red hair, though cut short, tumbled with its own fullness over an even-featured face with thin eyebrows atop her dark blue eyes. She had a straight, aquiline nose and lips that were nicely shaped, while not really full. She had the kind of milky white skin that so often went with orange-red hair. His eyes took in her tall, slender figure, the white shirt resting on longish breasts perhaps a little shallow at the tops, but nicely filled out below. Lean hips drew into long legs that tapered nicely under the skirt. As he took her in, he saw the coolness return to her eyes.

"It seems you can be competent when you're sober," she said.

"Competent? Is that all I was?" he snapped.

She let the coolness leave her eyes. "All right, a lot more than competent, I'll concede," she said.

"Damn right you will." Fargo grunted, peering at her. "Being nice is hard for you, isn't it?"

"Sometimes, especially when I'm given good reason not to be," she returned, bristling at once.

"I've come for my clothes," he stated gruffly. She turned, went over to the big bay, took Fargo's things from the saddlebag, and handed them to him.

"I was going to return them," she said tartly. "I didn't expect you'd be able to follow me."

"Aren't you lucky I was," Fargo said as her face softened, her cool good looks suddenly giving way to warm prettiness.

"Yes, I'm grateful for that. Really, I am," she said.

"You should be," he growled, his anger at her returning. "You know why those three came after you?"

She shrugged. "A woman riding alone. Easy pickings. That kind doesn't need more of a reason."

"Guess not," Fargo said.

"But you're thinking something else," she said, picking up on his tone quickly.

"Just wondering about the way they said things. One talked about getting rid of you as if that was first on their minds. Another said there was no reason they couldn't enjoy themselves, first," Fargo said.

13

She thought for a moment. "I didn't know them, never saw them before. I'd guess that was just their way of talking."

"You're probably right," he agreed. "You've a name?"

"Amity," she said. "Amity Baker."

"Amity," he repeated. "That sure as hell doesn't fit."

"Not when I'm cheated out of hard-earned money. Not when people get roaring drunk instead of keeping their word," she snapped.

He stepped back, took in the indignation in her face that held a lacing of disappointment with it. "Honey, you've got three minutes to tell me what the hell this is all about. Start talking fast," he said.

"Not here," she said, glancing at the three figures on the ground, a tiny shudder coursing through her. Turning, she pulled herself onto the Cleveland bay, mounting with a lithe, smooth motion that didn't even give sway to her breasts. He climbed onto the Ovaro and rode beside her as she went around to the other side of the pond, away from the three corpses, before she stopped. He slid to the ground with her. "You're a strange man, Fargo," she said, more perplexity than anger in her voice.

"That's been said before," he remarked dryly.

"You keep insisting you don't know why I came looking for you, yet you risked your life to save me," Amity Baker said.

"Call the last one a good deed. I don't know a damn thing about the first," Fargo said.

"You going to tell me you don't know Rufe Thomson?" Amity challenged, putting her hands on her slender hips.

Fargo's eyes narrowed at her with sudden caution. "No, I'm not going to tell you that," he said carefully.

"Good. Then you'll admit that he acts as an agent for you," she said.

Fargo felt the caution growing inside him. "From time to time," he said. "We go back a long ways, Rufe and I."

She reached into her skirt pocket, brought out a square of paper, and thrust it at him. He recognized Rufe's handwriting on it at once. "You going to try and deny that?" Amity flung at him. Fargo began to read the square of paper, already feeling the furrow cross his brow.

This will spell out the agreement between Miss Amity Baker of Green Hills, Minnesota, and Mr. Skye Fargo, generally known as the Trailsman, wherein Skye Fargo agrees, for the sum of one thousand dollars cash paid herewith, to break trail for the herd owned by Amity Baker.

Signed hereby for Skye Fargo by Rufe Thomson on this day of July 18, 1860.

Fargo noted Rufe's scrawling signature that followed, his frown now deeper on his brow as he handed the paper back.

"Well?" Amity demanded imperiously.

"Sometimes Rufe oversteps himself," Fargo began.

"He knew I'd just finished a job and was on my way to visit. You put down a powerful lot of money. I'd say he got carried away and tried to make everybody happy."

"When he wrote out this agreement he told me when to come back. I did, and somebody in his office directed me to your hotel room. I found you hardly fit to fulfill your commitment," Amity said reproachfully.

"I didn't make a commitment," Fargo said.

"Rufe Thomson made it for you," she countered.

"Rufe had no power to make it."

"You admitted he acted as an agent for you."

"I said he had from time to time, all on his own. He never had any right to. I just went along those other times," Fargo said.

"I'd like to hear what Rufe Thomson has to say about that," she snapped.

"Rufe's dead," Fargo said quietly, seeing Amity Baker's eyes grow wide and her lips drop open in shock.

"Oh, my. Oh, oh my," she breathed. "I'm sorry."

"Didn't know it myself till I rode in the day after it happened. He was killed in a holdup robbery in his office," Fargo said. "That's why I was in bed with a bottle of bourbon. Figured it'd help deal with the memories. As I said, Rufe and I went back a long time."

"I'm sorry. I had no idea. They just sent me back to the hotel room. I didn't know," Amity said.

"Now you do. I'm going back to finish remembering," Fargo said.

"You mean finish drinking," she said with instant reproach.

He shrugged. "A toast to remember, another to forget, and a couple to ask why. That's the way of it."

"You can't just walk away. I need your help. And I have an agreement," she protested.

"With a dead man who was wrong to make it in the first place. Sorry, honey," Fargo said and pulled himself onto the pinto.

"This isn't fair," she threw back angrily.

He paused, fastening her with a penetrating stare. "Fair? Who told you life was fair?" he said. "Ask Rufe about fair." He started to turn the pinto.

"Dammit, Fargo. I need you," she pleaded, and he saw the redheaded temper exploding inside her again. "You're being rotten."

"Think of those three varmints and say that again," he told her softly. Her curvaceous lips tightened and he saw remorse fighting with her temper.

"Go away," she murmured almost in a whisper.

"Amity's a nice name. Try living by it," he tossed back as he sent the pinto into a canter, feeling her eyes stay on him as he circled the pond and headed back to town. He kept a steady pace and found himself wondering if he'd seen the last of that carrot red hair.

2

Fargo scanned the countryside as he rode through the lengthening shadows of the afternoon, once again taking in the strength of the land in all its variety. It was a land that offered high forests and open plains, flat ranges, and rolling hills. The red men who reveled in its myriad of lakes, each a jewel of glistening blue, had named it Minnesota, the land where the sky is in the water. It was their land, they claimed, their birthright, and their home. The plains Ojibwa, the Winnebago, and the Saux-Fox had all retreated from their battles with the army, the fierce Indian Wars now a part of the bloody heritage that still stained the land.

Peace was an uncertain, fragile thing. Hate had deep roots. Riding through the land, savoring the brilliant scarlet banks of cardinal flowers and the yellow-and-white carpets of oxeye daisy, Fargo had the feeling that beauty itself could be a mask. The feeling was still with him when he reached Equity. He halted at the general store, enjoying the merchant's surprise when he paid for the clothes, then stopped at the stable and retrieved his saddle pouch. Back in his room at the hotel, he downed bourbon and stretched out on the bed as it all came rushing back over him again.

First, Rufe and his shock of unruly, white hair, his quick, all-encompassing grin. Fargo had known that smile for too many years, the grin of an old and faithful friend. Rufe Thomson had always tried to treat everyone honestly and fairly. He didn't deserve to be gunned down at the hands of callous, greedy killers. Fargo recalled riding into Equity only a few days ago, stopping at Rufe Thomson's little office on the main street. Charlie Hodd and Ben Derner had been there, along with a few more of Rufe's friends. They had quickly answered Fargo's angry questions. There had been four of the killers. They'd gunned down Rufe in cold blood, robbed the safe, and ran. One had dropped a casino chip from the big gaming house in Brown Hills, distinguishable by the house initials LL on it, for the Lucky Lady Casino. Someone had seen one who wore a tan Stetson with a red hatband as they ran to their horses. Another had a hat with a Montana pinch as all four had raced out of town together.

They would abide by their habits. They'd staged the holdup for the money, and they'd certainly be headed back to the gambling tables, Fargo was certain. He'd left Equity and headed for Brown Hills, a terrible anger churning inside him. It was dark when he'd reached Brown Hills, a town that consisted solely of the huge gaming house, two hotels, and a stable. He rode to the Lucky Lady, hitched the Ovaro outside, and entered the gambling den. The Lucky Lady consisted of one long, wide building with gambling tables from one end to the other. A bar took up the far wall, and girls in tights were busy running back and forth to the tables with drinks. Fargo saw a handful of men wandering the big room, plainly there to keep an eye on the players.

Fargo wandered through the cacophony of voices, glasses, the clink of ivory chips, and the smoke-filled haze in the air. He passed tables designated for black-jack, whist, twenty-one, poker, and dice. His eyes moved slowly from one table to another, watching not the gambling but the players as he swore softly to himself. Too many players had taken their hats off as they gambled, and on his second slow stroll around the huge room he stopped looking at the players and concentrated on the various hats hanging on the backs of the chairs. He took in Stetsons, bowlers, 'coon skin caps, ten-gallon hats, assorted short-brimmed caps, beaver and otter hats, straw fedoras, a few poblanos, and even a sombrero or two. He had reached a poker table in a far corner of the big room when he saw the tan Stetson, a red band around the base of the crown.

Fargo's eyes cut to the man in the chair, and saw a bulky figure with a hard face and a bulbous nose. The man held his cards close to his chest as another man, plainly a cohort, leaned down to whisper to him. Fargo quickly scanned the other four players, letting his eyes travel to the adjoining table, and found the hat with the four-sided Montana pinch hanging behind a lanky, long-faced man. Fargo stepped back, his eyes narrowed. He'd found three of them. The fourth was playing someplace close, he guessed. He felt his hand trembling as he held back from reaching for his gun.

He wanted to cut them down as mercilessly as they had Rufe. They didn't deserve any better. It would be easy enough to do, but his glance moved around the room. Many of those in the room were men who'd react instantly to gunfire. They'd come up shooting, fear or guilt triggering their reactions. All kinds of hell would break loose. The house guards would also react. Grimacing, Fargo backed away from the table, bought a drink from one of the girls in pink tights, and slowly sipped it as he watched the man with the tan Stetson. When the man finally went into a losing steak, Fargo finished his drink, then sauntered to the gaming house cashier. "Four five-dollar chips, please," he said and was given four white ivory chips with the distinctive double L on each. He pocketed the chips and returned to watch the man with the Stetson, seeing that he was giving up on his losing steak, muttering to his cohort beside him. Fargo moved away, strolled casually through the house, and left.

New customers were entering though it was well past midnight, Fargo noted as he walked the Ovaro across the street to a spot that let him see the gaming house entrance. Another half hour had passed when the chunky figure came through the doors, the tan Stetson on his head, his three fellow killers following close behind. Fargo's hand went to the Colt, but an oath fell from his lips—each of the four had a tights-clad girl from the gaming house on his arm. Fargo's hand stayed on the butt of the gun. In a shoot-out, any of the girls could take a fatal bullet, and he didn't want that. He wanted punishment to be specific, justice for only those who had killed in cold blood. His lips a tight line, Fargo watched the four men walk to the nearest of the two hotels and disappear inside.

He let a few minutes go by before he followed, entering the lobby of the hotel, a shabby, dimly lighted area with walls of peeling paint. A man in shirtsleeves stood up in a small cubicle just past the entranceway. He glanced at Fargo with bored eyes from a soft face entirely devoid of any character. "Room?" he asked.

"What rooms did you give the four men that just came in here with the girls?" Fargo asked.

"We don't give out that kind of information," the clerk said, managing to look affronted.

"I know, this is such a classy place," Fargo said sarcastically as he drew the Colt. "But you're going to make an exception, while you still can."

The man's eyes widened and he swallowed hard. "Rooms six, seven, eight, and nine," he said. "End of the hall."

"Smart man," Fargo said and treaded down the corridor, halting at a door marked with a number 6. He closed one hand around the doorknob, slowly turned the knob, and the door opened. A candle burned inside the small room, furnished with only a cot and a single straight-backed chair. The man was already naked, atop the girl who had also shed her tights, his hard-breathing grunts filling the room as he concentrated on pleasure. Fargo crossed the room on the balls of his feet, his arm quickly encircling the man's neck in a viselike grip as he pulled the man off of the girl beneath him. "Out, honey. Fast," Fargo said as terror filled her face. Her hand shot out from the cot, grabbed her tights, and she ran from the room with a brief flash of a tight little rear.

The man reared backward, tried to dislodge the figure holding him, but Fargo's arm tightened. Panic seizing hold of him, the man tried to twist himself around but Fargo's powerful arm constricted further. Gagging, the man twisted his neck again, and Fargo heard verterbrae snap. The man uttered a short, gurgling sound, then grew limp. Fargo stepped back and let the figure sink onto the cot, his head twisted to one side. He had really killed himself, Fargo realized. But it didn't matter. "One down, three to go," Fargo muttered as he spun and strode from the room.

Outside, he stepped to the next room, again carefully opening the door. The girl was on top this time, but Fargo recognized the chunky figure underneath her, and saw the tan Stetson beside the pile of clothes alongside the cot. He was by the cot in one long, silent stride, yanking the girl from off of the man and sending her sprawling on the floor. "This is a quickie. Out!" he spat at her, seeing her scramble for her outfit before running for the door. The man recovered from his surprise in time to kick out with both legs. Fargo turned, took the blow on one of his powerful thighs, and saw the man roll from the cot, reach into his clothes on the floor, and grab for his gun. Fargo skirted around the end of the cot, and brought the Colt down on the man's wrist. The man cursed in pain as the gun dropped from his hand. Fargo kicked the weapon away as the man dived into his pile of clothes once again, coming up with a long-bladed hunting knife.

He lunged forward, the knife thrust straight out before him. Fargo pulled his stomach in, seeing the knife go past him by a hair's breadth. As the man hurtled past him, Fargo brought his fist down in a pile-driver blow on the back of the man's neck. The chunky figure pitched face-forward to the floor with a shuddering groan, then he lay still. Fargo used one foot to push him onto his side and saw the knife imbedded to the hilt in his abdomen.

He turned, his jaw a tight line, and seconds later was at the third door. He knew exactly where the cot would be, now, the rooms being all exactly alike. Dismissing caution, he flung the door open and was beside the third cot in one stride. The naked man was the long-faced one who'd worn the hat with the Montana pinch. Fargo pressed the Colt into the back of his neck. "Hope you enjoyed it," he said. "It was your last one." Fargo saw the girl scuttle backward like a crab, her smallish breasts bouncing, as she pushed herself free of the man. "Take off," Fargo growled at her and she fell from the cot, grabbed her things, and ran for the door.

"What the hell is this?" The man glowered, still on his hands and knees on the cot.

"A message from Rufe Thomson," Fargo said, and the man fell silent in shock. Fargo pulled the Colt from his neck and stepped back. "I'm giving you a chance," he said, taking another step back. The man turned, and started to swing his legs from the cot.

"This ain't much of a chance," he complained.

"It's more than you gave Rufe," Fargo replied.

"I'm not going to try shooting it out with you, mister. Just let me put my pants on," the man whined.

Fargo held the grim smile inside himself. The man was trying to be crafty. "Why not," Fargo grunted. The man reached down, found his trousers, and started to draw them up. He was still bent over when Fargo saw his hand snap out, coming up with his pistol. He swung it up to fire from alongside the end of the cot, but the Colt barked first. The man's shot went into the wall as he pitched forward across the cot, almost in the same position he had been in when Fargo first came into the room.

Fargo whirled and ran from the room. The fourth one in the next room had heard the shot, of course. He'd be up, grabbing his gun, knowing only that there was trouble coming his way. Fargo reached the door of the adjoining room, dropped to the floor, and lay on his back. The Colt rested on his chest, poised forward to fire. Gathering powerful leg muscles, he kicked out with both feet and the door flew from its hinges. The man inside fired off a volley of shots, all intended for the figure he expected to be standing in the doorway. But all hurtled harmlessly over Fargo, who fired from his back into the room at the figure beside the cot. He saw the man's naked body jiggle comically as he fell forward to the floor, riddled with lead.

Fargo rose and stepped into the room. The naked, thin girl, sitting up on the cot and frozen in place, stared up at him in terror, looking pitifully vulnerable.

"Get dressed, honey. You're through for the night," he said, turning to leave as she frantically pulled on her tights. He walked down the hallway to where the desk clerk had flattened himself against the wall of his cubicle. The man cringed as Fargo approached. Taking the four white gaming chips from his pocket, Fargo positioned the ivory squares in a row, standing each on its end atop the registration desk counter. "They'll be hurrying over from the Lucky Lady," Fargo said.

"Yes, sir. I expect so," the clerk agreed.

Fargo gestured to the four gaming chips. "What do you think these are?" he asked.

"Gaming chips," the clerk offered hesitantly.

"Wrong," Fargo said. "Guess again."

"I . . . I don't know," the man said nervously.

"They're headstones," Fargo said. "One for each of the rotten, stinking bastards down the hall, courtesy of Rufe Thomson. Tell that to anyone who asks." The man nodded and Fargo left, riding out of the poor excuse of a town that was Brown Hills. It was morning when he'd arrived back in Equity, just in time for Rufe's funeral. He'd brought an unseen spectator to the ceremony—justice—and was glad he had. Rufe deserved no less.

Memories snapped off inside the darkness of Fargo's mind once he was back in his hotel room. It was over, everything finished including the bourbon, everything beyond changing, another example that life was full of strange twists and turns. He closed his eyes and let sleep tune out the harsh, waking world.

3

The night staved off the waking world until the morning sun flooded into Fargo's room. He lay awake a little longer but finally rose and went to the dresser. A new pitcher had replaced the shattered one, now filled with fresh water. He used the pearlash soap the hotel provided to wash. Finally dressed, he left the room, paid his bill, and retrieved the Ovaro at the public stable. He stopped to have a cup of coffee at a small bake shop run by a pleasant-faced woman in a white apron. Leaning against a pole outside, he had just begun to sip the coffee when he saw the flash of carrot red hair coming across the street toward him.

He faced Amity with an apprehensive stare as she halted beside him. "Coffee with milk," she said to the woman.

"You come looking for trouble, again?" Fargo asked her. "You'll find it. My head still hurts."

"Bourbon or the pitcher?" she questioned.

"Both," he snapped as he peered at her, not seeing any apology in her dark azure eyes.

"Didn't come looking for trouble. I came to get what's due me," she said.

"According to you," Fargo said with a growl.

She summoned earnestness into her face. "Spent the night thinking about this," Amity Baker said. "I'm very sorry about what happened to Rufe Thomson, but I shouldn't be penalized for it."

"Nobody's doing that," Fargo said between sips of coffee.

"You are," she snapped, her temper flaring. "The agreement was made in your name. It's your place to fulfill it."

"That's called being hard-nosed." Fargo grunted.

"That's called need," she threw back, drawing deeply on her coffee. "I paid Rufe Thomson a thousand dollars."

"Money that was stolen," Fargo reminded her.

"Money I can't replace. I don't have another thousand dollars. Do you have it to give back to me?" she pushed at him.

"Nope," Fargo said.

"Then I expect you to honor my agreement. It's the only fair thing, the only *just* thing," she said, managing to sound reproachful as she finished her coffee.

Fargo's lips tightened. She had more than a good case. She was a victim, just as Rufe had been. None of it had been her fault. He wouldn't deny that, and he couldn't be stiff-backed about it. That would be less than honest, and Fargo had to admire the way she fought for her stand. "Let's ride some," he said as he drained the coffee and climbed onto the Ovaro, waiting as she got her big bay and swung alongside him. He led the way out of Equity and across terrain of soft grama grass and fragrant leaves of black walnut. He glanced at her, seeing the way she rode with easy grace, her long figure moving in rhythm with her horse, her breasts swaying gently from side to side. "Along with that red-head temper, you don't back down easily, do you?" he commented.

"Not when I'm right," she said. "And you know I'm right."

"What makes you so sure that I'll go along with you?" He half smiled.

"Because you can't help yourself," she said with a hint of smugness.

"How do you figure that?" He frowned.

"Anyone who would risk their life for me the way you did must have a sense of right and wrong," she said, plainly pleased with herself.

"That's kind of a roundabout way of thinking," he said.

"Tell me I'm wrong. Say it," she challenged, and he swore inwardly. He wouldn't bow to her challenge, but he couldn't step on his own integrity, either. She had a way of daring you to choose one or the other. He halted under the branches of a wide walnut tree, heavy with hard-shelled nuts, and swung from the pinto. Amity dismounted and faced him, her eyes waiting.

"Looking at it one way, you're right, you're owed. None of what happened was your fault," he began.

"Then you'll help me, you'll stand by the agreement," she said, leaping to what she wanted to hear.

"No," he said. "It's not that I wouldn't want to. I just can't," he said.

Angry impatience flooded her face. "That's ridiculous. Why can't you?" she threw back.

"There's something else I have to do, a commitment, you could say," he answered, taking her by the arm and pulling her down under the tree with him. "Rufe didn't know about it when he signed that agreement."

Her eyes shot back skepticism. "What kind of commitment?"

"I guess it's not just a commitment. More like an order," he said.

"An order?" she frowned. "From who?"

"The United States Army, specifically General Miles Davis of the Fifth U.S. Cavalry," Fargo said. Her frown remained as she stared at him. "He sent for me. I've done things for Miles before, some official assignments, others quite unofficial."

"What is it all about?" Amity questioned, suspicion still clouding her voice.

"I don't know," he said.

"You don't know?" she returned, throwing up her hands in exasperation. "I'm supposed to believe that?"

"He didn't give me details. He won't till I get there," Fargo told her. "But it's important. He wouldn't contact me for ordinary small stuff. General Davis is one of the army's good people, a top commander."

Amity folded her arms across her breasts as her eyes bored into him. "It all still comes out one way. I'm getting shafted, twice. Once by a gang of holdup men and now by the U.S. Army," she said crossly.

He grimaced at her accuracy. "Can't say you're wrong. Guess you could add me onto that list."

The anger dissolved in her face with startling suddenness as she put her hands on his chest. "No, I won't be doing that, not after you saved my neck. I guess maybe we're both just caught up in the same thing," she said.

"That's a good way of seeing it," he agreed. "Shows you can exercise something besides that temper."

She leaned over and her lips touched his, a sweet, almost shy kiss, and she pulled its warmth back quickly.

"Proving you can live up to your name?" He smiled.

"Just saying thank you for yesterday," she said.

"We'd better ride. I'm expected," Fargo said, pulling her to her feet with him. She came easily, her body a controlled lightness made of natural grace.

"Where are you meeting General Davis?" she asked.

"At Fort Comber along the Buffalo River," Fargo said.

"That's on the way to where my herd is waiting, east of Osage," Amity said. "We could ride together. We'd reach the herd by morning. I'd like you to see it."

He smiled. "You wouldn't try to convince me of anything along the way, would you?"

"Not the way you're thinking," she snapped at once.

"Why not?" He laughed.

She regarded him with a long, thoughtful glance. "It'd be a waste of time," she said. "Not that you'd turn away from a little friendly persuasion, but you're not the kind to be bought."

"Bull's-eye." He laughed. "And you're not really the kind to offer friendly persuasion."

31

"Bull's-eye," she echoed tartly. "Guess that makes us even on that score. Now, are we going to ride together?"

"Why not?" he said as she pulled herself onto the big bay. "I'd much rather ride beside a beautiful woman than alone."

"Beautiful?" She laughed, a soft, warm sound. "Never been called that before."

"Maybe because you're all riled up and crabby too often," he suggested.

She laughed again. "No, it's because I'm not the soft cuddly kind men take to," she answered.

"You work hard at not being that," he answered, but not harshly.

"It just happened that way. My pa was alone, and a very sick man the last ten years of his life. He worked with me as much as he could, taught me a whole lot, but I was pretty much on my own. That makes you someone who has to stand up for yourself," Amity said.

"Having a temper to go with that hair helps, too," he said wryly, but Fargo felt a new understanding toward her. Amity Baker was a cut apart from the average young woman, he decided as he put the pinto into a trot. The sun began to slant its late-afternoon rays along the deep green of the forests. He led the way through fields of soft gold foxtail barley and purple-rose prairie clover and when dusk came, they found a spot beside a swift-flowing stream. Amity offered some tasty dried beef strips made with a mixture of sugar and buffalo berry, and the cool stream water was like sweet nectar.

It was soon night, the sky a deep blue cloth speckled with silver sequins, and Fargo set out his bedroll, undressed to his underdrawers, and lay down. Amity came back from the bay with a blanket, wearing a short, cotton nightgown that let him see her long, shapely calves and nicely rounded knees. She lay her blanket down half over the side of his bedroll and sat down beside him, her eyes lingering over the muscled contours of his body. "I really want you to see the herd. They're special," she said.

"That's what most say about their herds," he observed.

"Mine *are*," she said emphatically. "I've a crew of young cowhands watching them. We ought to reach them by midmorning." She turned, and brought herself closer to him. "You'll be taking off after you see them. I've no wild misconceptions about that."

"Good," he said.

"But I want you to know I'll never forget yesterday. No one ever did anything like that for me before," Amity said.

"Maybe they never had the chance," he suggested.

"I don't expect they would if they had," she said.

"Maybe you shouldn't be so cynical," Fargo replied. "Maybe you ought to give people a chance. They might surprise you."

"I've seen enough, watched enough. It's not being cynical, just realistic," she said, and then leaned forward and brought her lips to his, and he felt the same sweet, shy kiss. She didn't pull away as quickly this time. He felt the tips of her breasts touch his chest, a soft, barely perceptible pressure. When she pulled back, she peered at her.

"Thought you weren't going to try convincing me," he said.

"I'm not," she said.

"What was that?" he questioned.

"Saying thank you, again. Saying I'll always be grateful. You reach a person, Fargo. You just do, in one way or another," she said.

"Should I be apologizing for that?" He smiled.

"No," she said. "Just understand it. Good night," she added abruptly, then turned on her side and lay still. He lay back and closed his eyes. Amity Baker was not an experienced young woman, yet she had something that perhaps more than made up for experience, a quick sensitivity that let her know people in her own, shortcut way. It could help her in life. Or hurt her, Fargo mused. It could let her see things she might not want to see, prevent her from looking away when that was the best thing to do. His thoughts continued to idle as he felt her move, her back now resting against his as her breathing fell into the steady rhythm of sleep. He went to sleep with her warm softness against him.

He awoke twice during the night, once to the howl of timber wolves and once to the closer growls of black bears, and found Amity still sleeping against him. When morning came, he awoke first, and went to wash in the steam. When he returned, he found Amity up and awake. She held her blanket to her as she trudged to the big bay and the stream. When she returned, she wore a green shirt that made her vibrant carrot red hair leap out in contrast. He found a stand of red mulberry for them to breakfast on before taking to the saddle. "Sleep well?" he asked mildly.

"Very," she said primly, her face expressionless, and he smiled inwardly. She had retreated from the spontaneous warmth of the previous night, but Fargo could sense her excitement grow as they swung east along the White Earth River. It was midmorning when he spied the distant mass of cattle spread out in a loose circle. Amity put her horse into a canter and Fargo followed, drawing alongside her as they grew closer to the herd. A furrow crossed his brow, becoming a deep frown when they reached the herd. Amity reined up, and walked the big bay on to talk to three of her hands. They were hardly more than boys, Fargo saw with a quick glance, his eyes instantly returning to the herd. He stared at cattle, which were unlike any he had ever seen, and dismounted, approaching the steers on foot. His gaze took in the blocky, sturdy steers with medium length horns. Most striking though was the very shaggy, thick coat on each steer, both on the calves and the mature animals. Long, often flat-lying mantles of long, somewhat stringy, wool-like fleece covered each of the mature animals so they looked as though someone had draped an extra coat over them. Without the cumbersomeness of Herefords or guernseys, they were nonetheless powerful, solid cattle and their shaggy appearance gave them a somewhat belligerent mien. He was still studying them in fascination when Amity's voice sounded beside him.

"Scotch Highland cattle," she said. "Never seen anything like them, have you?"

"Sure as hell not," he agreed.

"Pa and I bred them from stock brought over here from Scotland by boat. They're fine cattle and they're needed here," Amity said. "They've great things to offer."

"Such as?"

"They're hardy, disease resistant, thrive on grass, forage, or other harsh land, and they mature faster than many breeds. But mostly, they're needed to keep the livestock population balanced. We're only developing a few strains here. If any one of them are hit by a particular disease, we're in trouble. Those damn longhorns that are all over the southwest are an example. Besides being rotten-tempered, coarse-haired, flat-sided and mostly horns and hooves, they carry Texas fever to other breeds. The same thing could happen all over. That's why a variety of livestock type is so important."

"You're talking about educating ranchers to a different way of thinking. That won't be easy," Fargo said.

"Maybe not, but if it isn't done, someday we'll all be sorry," Amity said.

"Someday?"

"Maybe twenty-five years, maybe fifty, a hundred, even two hundred years, but the more we lose species diversity the worse off we'll be," she said.

"You want to fill that out some for us ordinary folk?" Fargo said.

"Different species or breeds have different things to offer. They have strengths in their makeup, their blood, if you like, that are important to keep. If we develop only one strain, we open ourselves to all kinds of dangers. It doesn't just go for cattle. It holds for everything—pigs, chickens, sheep, trees, plants, wheat, corn, anything you can name. We breed only one kind of plant or wheat, one species of chicken, we'll be weakening the strain. That's what my Scotch Highland cattle have to offer—strength and new blood."

Fargo's eyes traveled slowly across the herd. "They have an unusual coat. Can it stand up to the bitter cold of plains winters?"

"We've taken them through two winters already," Amity said.

His glance was slightly chiding. "In barns, I'll bet. With food and shelter. They weren't left out on the range to fend for themselves, were they?"

Her shrug was an admission. "We were raising them. They were very valuable so we protected them. But I know the history of the breed. They're hardy. There are hard winters in Scotland."

"No winters are like the western plains or Canadian winters," Fargo said.

"My cattle will do fine," Amity said firmly, though he thought he detected more self-assurance than certainty. "I'm not the only one who believes in them," she added.

"Your buyer, of course," Fargo said.

"His name's Royce Cantwell. He's contracted to buy the whole herd, except for a few calves I've kept back at my place. I'm taking him the rest," Amity said.

"Taking them where?"

"To his spread. It's along the Moose River, east of Thief Lake."

Fargo's lips pursed. "That's way up in the north

country. That'll be a rough trip. He's paying you good money, I take it."

"Top dollar on delivery," Amity said and her hands came to rest against his chest. "You see why I need you to break trail for me. I want the herd delivered the quickest and best way I can. Sure, the money is important, but there's more than money involved."

"Such as?"

"Faith, vindication, the gamble that was taken. I appreciate Royce Cantwell's decision to buy. He's gambling, too, having faith just as I had when I began to breed old strains that need preserving. When I began to work with my pa we had to have confidence and we had to be willing to gamble. You have to believe in the merit and the justification to raise Scotch Highland, or any old breed, to raise them. If I'm right, Royce Cantwell will have the inside track on a new breed that can sweep the market, and I'll have brought something really important to the country."

"Hope you're right. That's what dreams are made of," Fargo said.

"You don't need to have my faith. All you need is to bring your special talents and break trail for me," Amity said with a warm, wide smile as she slid her arms around his shoulders. "I knew once you saw them you'd see this is not an ordinary cattle drive, and no ordinary herd."

"I see that, Amity, and I'll help you. But I can't till I meet with General Davis," he said.

Her face fell. "You don't know what he wants or how

long it'll take," she said. "Time is important to me. I can't sit around waiting."

He grimaced inwardly and felt for her frustration and despair. "I'll make you the only promise I can. Maybe what Miles wants won't take long, maybe only a week or so," he said, yet he knew he was being less than realistic. Still, there was always an off-chance. "When I'm finished I'll come back and break trail for you. This is good land. The herd can hang out here until I get back."

Her eyes searched his face. "A week. You make it sound like nothing. A week can be a long time," Amity said.

"It's the only promise I can give you. I'll come back," he said.

"It's not what I'd hoped to hear," she said.

"You'd no right to expect more," he said gently. She didn't answer, just turned her face away, her lips tight. He leaned over, kissed her cheek, and pulled himself onto the Ovaro. This was a time when words seemed superfluous. He rode away slowly and felt the silent accusation she sent after him. He didn't blame her, couldn't even fault her. She was a victim of circumstances, but she was also a determined, angry young woman with her own set of priorities. He wouldn't make them his, wouldn't and couldn't. Miles Davis never cried wolf.

Fargo put the pinto into a trot. He had made his plans before he'd ever heard of Amity Baker. Empathy had its limits.

4

The sun was nearing the horizon when Fargo passed the Sand Hill River where it curved south. The land grew flat with quaking aspen dotting the terrain, their waxy buds glowing with a silvery sheen in the late sun. When he rode into the low dip of land, the field met his eye at once, well tended with long, low rows of rich soil. Under each row were potatoes, growing fat in the good soil. Fargo headed for the modest frame and shingle house at the end of the field, passing four figures pulling up potatoes to toss into big burlap sacks on the ground. Reining up in front of the house, Fargo dismounted and took in the two long storage sheds only a few feet from the house.

He had tethered the pinto when a woman came from one of the sheds holding a small basket of potatoes. A one-piece, loose gray dress covered her large frame, and she halted, staring at him as she dropped the basket. "By God! I don't believe it," she breathed and then she was running full-tilt at him. He was braced and ready when she flung herself into his arms with exuberant ferocity. "Skye . . . Skye Fargo," she squealed and clung to him.

"Lucy Crawford," he returned and she loosened her hold of him and drew back enough for him to take in her round, pleasant face, full lips and plump cheeks, brown eyes and light brown hair falling across an open, inviting face. "You look great, Lucy," he said.

"Ten pounds more of me to look great," she said.

"Doesn't hurt any," Fargo said, words that were made of truth, not politeness. Lucy had always been a roundish girl back in Missouri, never fat but always pleasantly padded, her body round, a deep spring of rib and a plump rear. But she had always carried it well, outdoing girls with more perfect figures. Probably, he had always suspected, because she so enjoyed being herself, thoroughly open and without pretensions. Things hadn't changed in that regard, he noted as her mouth came to his, lingering, then finally drawing back.

"God, I'm not dreaming," Lucy said.

"I wrote you I might be stopping by," Fargo said.

"You've done that before. Didn't put a lot of hope in it," she said and led him into the house, where he found a comfortable, modest living room with vases of daffodils along the fireplace mantel. Memories rushed over him, back to when Lucy and her folks had a small farm in Missouri and Lucy worked as a barmaid at a local pub. He remembered how she had always been friendly yet selective, and how they had instantly hit it off together. It had been a good relationship from the start, simple and uncluttered, and he'd visited after every trip until she'd gone to Minnesota with her folks, when time and distance took its toll. He had learned that the potato farm had done well and when her folks died, she's stayed on to run it.

She cut off the memories as she pulled him into a bedroom with a large bed and a pink sheet over it, going over to light the lamp as dusk began to darken the room. "You know what I've told myself all these nights, Fargo?" Lucy asked and didn't wait for an answer. "I promised myself that if you ever came visiting I'd have you in bed before five minutes passed, no matter where or when. Five minutes is almost up."

"Wouldn't want you to break a promise," Fargo said. She lifted her arms, whisked the dress over her head, then the half-slip beneath it, shimmied out of her white bloomers and faced him, her head held high with a kind of defiant pride. She had a right, he saw, her round, cream white breasts still full and firm, not a hint of pull or sag, each nipple just as he remembered, a small but thrusting pink tip on an equally small pink areola. Her rib cage, always deep, carried the extra few pounds invisibly, and her little belly was the convex mound it had always been. It curved downward to the small but bushy triangle that offered the same provocative invitation.

Her thighs, as always, were a trifle plump, but not without shape. There was a beauty in her sturdiness, he had realized long ago. But above all, Lucy radiated the same simple happiness in the prospect and pleasure of making love as she always had. It was in the smile that wreathed her face, in the way her arms opened up to draw him to her, and the way she eagerly helped him shed his clothes. "I've waited so damn long for you to visit, dreamt about it so often," she murmured. His clothes tossed aside, Fargo felt the wonderful softness of her as she pressed her creamy breasts against him.

The excited eagerness of yesterdays flowed up to roll over them both as Fargo's lips found one full breast, drew it into his mouth, then moved on to the other, caressing each with his tongue as Lucy shuddered as she moaned. She pushed against him, sliding her roundness up and down his body, little caresses of the skin, overtures of arousal. Her belly pressed into his groin as she rubbed back and forth again. "Skye . . . Skye . . . oh, yes, yes," she breathed as she pressed harder. She positioned her breast inside his mouth as if she wanted to feel every last spot of pleasure, absorb every inch of sensation. He heard her little sighs, a core of pure delight nestled in each one, and again he knew the sheer, open delight in pleasure that was Lucy. Little squeals, half laughs, exuberant little cries, they all poured from her, part of the special enjoyment that was Lucy. No sultry, smoky heavings from her, only marvelous, sweeping enthusiasm. Lucy was like love with laughter, sex with sunshine.

His hand reached down, traveled across her warm, smooth body, enjoying the seamlessness of her and she cried out at his touch. When he reached her black, bushy mound, he pushed his hand through the soft hairs, and little tendrils rose up to curl around his fingers possessively. "Oh, yes, yes, yes." Lucy gasped, pushing her pelvis upward as her legs lifted, falling open for him, the eternal invitation offered without words. Her hands were clasped around his buttocks, pulling him to her and he felt the dampness of her thighs cling against him.

He moved forward slowly, finding her dark, sweet portal, a lubricious touch of pleasure. Lucy's cry spiraled in the dimness of the room. "Yes, oh, oh, yes, yes, yes." She gasped and moved with him, her body rising and falling, turning and twisting, emitting little screams of unfettered pleasure. She pulled his head down and buried his face into her breasts as her hips rose and thrust upward to meet his surges. Her creamy mounds encompassing him, he reveled in her cries of delight, responded to the pure joy of her entire being. Wonderful nights relegated to memory returned as he found himself swept up in Lucy's total and complete enthusiasm, her towering *joie de vivre* of the spirit. When he felt her flesh draw back for a moment, then slap hard against him, her voice rising to a cry of ecstasy wrapped in laughter, he let himself go with her, his wanton throbbing matching her explosion of happy triumph.

She held him hard to her, her breasts pushed against his face, their small, firm tips demanding to rest in his mouth, and he trembled with her as the night split open, and allowed the fleeting moment of supreme ecstasy to reign. It seemed to linger longer than usual, the fates joining Lucy in smiling on her moment of pleasure recaptured. But as always, the moment spiraled away to leave the senses only with the embers of the incomparable, and he felt Lucy relax against him, sinking down on the bed. "Oh, damn," he heard her murmur with more resignation than anger. He held her, enjoying the still-throbbing heat of her against him, the damp softness of her Venus mound pressing into his groin.

Finally, she lay back, her smile quietly triumphant. "As wonderful as always," she said softly.

"It was," he agreed.

"But then I knew it would be," Lucy said, rising up on one elbow and looking soft and lovely. "There's good day-old stew in the kettle. It'll restore your strength for later," she said.

"Sounds good to me," he said. "What about your help? I saw some hands picking in the field."

"They're done with their chores. They're on their way home by now. That's how I've arranged things. I like it better than help living on the place," she said, swinging from the bed and pulling open the kitchen curtains as she started to heat a big, black iron kettle. She put on an apron which barely covered her groin as he sat back and watched her prepare supper and set the table. There was none of the sultry vamp in Lucy now, only her open, laughing, natural self which, he realized as he watched her, sent out its own kind of unvarnished sexuality. She brought out a bottle of good rye whiskey and they talked about old times. The supper was quickly finished and he found himself lying beside Lucy in her pink-sheeted bed. "You wouldn't be staying awhile, would you?" she asked hopefully, resting against him.

"Can't," he said with honest rue.

"Expected that. Just thought I'd ask," she said.

"The army's called me in," he told her. "Stopping here was on my way."

"I'll take any reason." Lucy laughed, and swung herself over him, her lips finding his. Her hand reached down and found more of him and her stroking and caressing made her own body hot at once. All her wonderful, waiting passion erupted again in all the special dimension she brought to it. In minutes, her cries of delight filled the room. She was atop him now, bouncing up and down with fervent pleasure, when the door of the room suddenly flew open.

Fargo peered past Lucy's shoulder at the figure in the doorway, the shock of red hair glowing in the candlelight. He saw the fury in her face, then the big carbine in her hands. "General Davis?" Amity bit out at Lucy. "You don't look like a general, leastwise not one I've ever met." Fargo saw the carbine come up, the shot exploding in the small confines of the room as it blasted a hole in the wall over the top of the bed. He threw Lucy from the bed, following her as they hit the floor as another shot blasted, this one sending the sheet and mattress exploding in a shower of pink shreds and feathers. "Sleep on that with the general, damn you," Amity screamed.

"Dammit, girl!" Fargo shouted, starting to pull himself up, but then diving back to the floor as the carbine erupted again. The foot of the bed came apart in splinters and shards.

"Liar! Damn liar," he heard Amity shout, something much more than fury catching in her voice. He raised his head to see her running from the doorway, then he heard her storm from the house, and seconds later the sound of galloping hoofbeats resounded in the night. Fargo pushed to his feet, pulling Lucy up with him.

"Sorry about this," he muttered. "She's got a rotten temper."

"That's plain to see," Lucy said dryly, pulling on a robe and lowering herself to the edge of the shattered bed, giving him a sideways glance. "You want to tell me about it?" she asked. Fargo's lips pulled back as he sat down beside her, telling her about Rufe Thomson, Amity's agreement, and her cattle. Lucy's lips were pursed in thought when he finished. "Rotten turn of things for her," Lucy said.

"That's true enough," Fargo agreed.

"And now she thinks you just lied to her, played her along," Lucy said.

"Nobody told her to follow me. That's what she gets for being suspicious. She can stay mad." Fargo frowned.

"She's not just angry," Lucy said evenly. "She's hurt. She feels betrayed. And it's personal."

"What's that mean?" Fargo tossed back.

"She likes you, maybe a lot, probably more than she should. You did something to make that happen," Lucy said.

"I saved her neck." Fargo grunted.

"That's enough, and you let her think you understood her, believed in her," Lucy added.

47

"I suppose so," Fargo conceded. "I did sympathize."

"And now she's pretty damn shattered. You ought to go after her, straighten this out," Lucy said.

He frowned at her. "You're being too goddamn forgiving. She shot your bedroom up," he said.

"I'm thinking how I'd feel in her place. I'd be real hurt, too, and she's ten years younger than me," Lucy said.

"You'd be hurt, but you wouldn't damn near kill somebody," he growled.

"I don't have her red hair," Lucy replied. "Everybody has their own ways of being hurt. Besides, I'm not just talking for her." Fargo frowned at her and she came closer, putting her arms around him. "I'm telling you to do what's right for you. I've known you too long and too well, Skye Fargo. You can't leave things hanging wrong. It's not in you. It'll keep eating at you. Go after her, straighten it out. She's owed that much."

His arms encircled Lucy, his eyes probing into hers. "If I go all the way back after her, I won't have time to stop by again. I'll have to be on my way to Miles Davis," he said.

"You came. We had these hours together. I'll have to keep remembering till next time. I've gotten good at that," Lucy said. Her lips pressed against his, her soft sweetness spreading warmth, and they traded a rueful smile. She was right, of course. He'd eat himself up if he let Amity go on wrapped in her own hurts, holding all the wrong things inside her.

"You're something special, Lucy Crawford," he said as he held her tight.

"Get dressed while I'm still feeling noble," she returned. He reached for his clothes and when he finished dressing, she clung to him a moment longer, a hint of regret in her eyes.

"I'll be visiting again. That's a promise," he said.

"I'll have the bed fixed by then," she said and waved him out the door.

He put the Ovaro into an easy pace. Amity would have ridden hard, forcing her horse as fury drove her. He wouldn't make an effort to catch up to her. It would only exhaust the Ovaro and there was no need. Amity would reach the herd in the morning, as much tuckered out as the big bay. She and her horse would both need rest and he guessed she'd have to spend most of the day sleeping. He had no reason to race after her. Besides, he didn't want to come upon her by day. She'd still be fuming. She might well start using the carbine again, her temper erupting at the sight of him. He realized she'd purposely missed at Lucy's place, but by damn little. Next time her shots could get away from her. He'd not risk a bullet because of hasty shooting.

"I'll wait till dark to confront Amity," he muttered to himself and held the pinto to a nice, steady pace. When dawn came, he found a place to rest in a thicket of shadbush and slept most of the day. When he awoke, he freshened himself and the Ovaro at a lake and continued on. Dusk was descending when he finally neared the herd. A low hill, well covered with hackberry and profuse growths of wavy-leafed, three-foot-tall yellow dock, rose up at one side of where the herd grazed. Fargo dismounted, led the pinto up the low part of the hill, and halted where he could look down at the camp in the gathering dusk. It wasn't hard to spot Amity's carrot top head even in the twilight. He waited, watching the hands change shifts for the oncoming night, the day hands trudging off with their bedrolls. He saw Amity retire into a pup tent set up at one edge of the herd, almost at the base of the low hill, and he settled back, giving her time to prepare for sleep.

The night swept down quickly and when he'd let enough time go by, he rose, tethered the Ovaro to a low branch, and started down the hill on foot, picking his way by the light of a half-moon. The herd was quiet, only the occasional bellow sounding through the night. He was too small a presence for them to smell and too quiet for them to hear. When he reached the bottom of the hill he continued on soundless, careful steps, circling the edge of the herd, taking in the nearest cowhand quietly sitting his horse. Fargo crept on until he reached the small tent, then he dropped to one knee and put his ear to the edge of the tent flap. The sounds of her steady breathing came to him as he lifted the flap and squeezed inside the tent where the moonlight came in from a hole in the top to afford ample light.

Amity lay on her blanket on the floor of the tent, two traveling bags nearby and the carbine at the edge of the blanket. He dropped to one knee beside her, and closed one hand over her mouth. She snapped awake at once, eyes wide with alarm, then surprise. "I'm going to take my hand away," he said. "You promise you won't start screaming, shouting, or shooting?"

Her eyes bored into him and he saw the thoughts racing through her head. Finally, she nodded. He took his hand from her mouth and she sat up instantly, her breasts bouncing under the sheer nightshirt she wore. "What are you doing here?" she hissed.

"Came to talk," he said.

She glared at him. "I don't talk to liars."

"Then you can just listen," he said calmly.

"I don't listen to liars, either," Amity snapped.

"I didn't lie to you," Fargo said.

"Hah!" She snorted and then, mimicking, threw his words back at him with bitter sarcasm. "You shouldn't be cynical. You ought to give people a chance."

"That's right," he returned. "You couldn't do that. You had to follow me. You think you found out something but you didn't."

"I found out some generals have big boobs," she flung back.

"Dammit, Amity Baker, you listen to me. I'm on my way to see General Davis. That's no lie. I told you the truth. I just left out a little," he said.

"A little screwing, you mean," she said hotly.

Fargo refused to sound apologetic. "Lucy Crawford's an old friend. I stopped to see her on my way to Miles Davis. That's the whole damn truth of it."

Her burning stare continued to spear into him. "Why in heaven's name should I believe a word of this?" she asked.

"Because I'm here," he said simply and saw the answer catch as she peered at him, her forehead taking on a wrinkle. "Think, dammit," he said. "Put a hold on that damn temper of yours. I could have stayed with Lucy. Liars aren't bothered by conscience. Why would I come all the way back here?"

She thought another moment, her eyes still on him. "I don't know. Why did you come back?" she asked.

"Because I know what you'd go on thinking and I didn't want that, not for you and not for myself," he said honestly. "I didn't lie to you about having to go see Miles Davis. I just left out Lucy. There's a difference."

"I suppose there is," she conceded. "Can't say I think much of it, though," she added tartly, but he saw her fury begin to drain. He waited and she glowered back. "You expect me to say thank you for coming back?" she said.

"No, that'd be too much to ask of you. Just believe me. I'll settle for that," he answered.

"Now what?" she questioned. "You didn't come back to stay and break trail for me. I'm in the same boat."

"But you feel better." He smiled. "You know you do." Her silence was a kind of admission, though she held on to her glower. "Look, I came to tell you I'll come back and break trail for you. That's a promise. Just hold out here till then," he said.

"I can't. You could be too long coming back. I'm going to have to go on myself."

"You ever break trail?" he asked and she shook her head. "You'll do better to wait," he said.

"I can't. I've seven hands, eight counting me. I'll have to go on. Time's too important," she said.

He shrugged and knew he had no words that would stop her. Maybe she's already lost enough time making mistakes to halt and wait. "Are we still friends?" he asked, taking her arm.

"Guess so," she muttered, "seeing as how you did come all the way back."

"Then I'll be going on to see Miles," Fargo said.

"With another detour at Lucy's?" she slid at him, disapproval in her tone.

"No," he said. "Follow me if you want." She wrinkled her nose at him as he slipped from the tent. Outside, he dropped into a stoop, there being no point in being seen by the hands. Moving in a low, loping crouch, he circled the edge of the herd, and had just begun to climb the low hill when he heard the cattle suddenly grow restless. They moved in place, shuffling their hooves, and then one bellowed, followed by another until there was a chorus of bellows that quickly grew louder. Restlessness was a contagion. It spread from one to the other as Fargo saw the cowhands quickly move along the edges of the herd, trying to calm the animals by their familiar presence.

But the herd continued to be jittery despite the hands calling to them soothingly. Fargo began to move up the low hill through the hackberry and the thick, yellow dock, the lowing of the cattle loudly reaching up to him. Something had set them off, Fargo was sure, and he was halfway to where he'd left the Ovaro when he halted. The odor drifted to him from across the hill, the dark, dank pungency of it unmistakable as it lit up his nostrils and his memory. He'd picked it up,

53

just as readily as the cattle had. It was enough to set them off, something strange and disturbing, permeating the dark gloom.

Fargo's nostrils flared as he drew in the odor and, turning, he began to follow his nose. It led him across the hill to the other side, growing stronger as it did. Then he saw the lone rider moving slowly down the hill in the hackberry. Fargo shifted direction, following as he saw the rider halt some hundred or so yards from the base of the hill. He dismounted and Fargo saw that he was at a spot where he could edge down along the herd and come out at Amity's tent. Fargo drew his Colt and immediately holstered it again as he swore softly. Touched by the moonlight, the man would be easy to bring down with a clean shot, but that same shot would be enough to send the herd into an all-out, flying stampede. The few hands in the saddle would be totally helpless to stop the herd as they raced off in all directions. Amity would be lucky to get twenty-five percent of them back.

Fargo swore again and hurried forward as the figure neared the tent. In the man's hand, glinting in the moonlight, the blade of a hunting knife showed itself. Fargo went into a run, letting the bellowing of the cattle cover the sound of his footsteps. He reached the bottom of the hill as the man slipped into the tent through the flap. Racing full-out, Fargo crashed into the tent and saw the man standing above Amity, who lay in her blanket. His arm was raised to bring the knife down. He turned as Fargo came hurtling into the tent but Fargo was already diving, smashing into the man at the knees and sending him sprawling backward. Amity woke, gave a piercing scream and out of the corner of his eye Fargo saw her roll from the blanket. Lashing out with a looping left, Fargo grazed the man's jaw with a blow but the man twisted aside, and came back with a vicious, sweeping slash with the knife. Fargo managed to duck beneath it but the man followed through, slashing out again with the blade. Fargo twisted away and glimpsed Amity. She had seized the carbine and was bringing it up to blast the man.

"No!" Fargo shouted, and saw Amity's eyes widen in surprise. But the man understood, an evil grin cracking his face as he leaped at Fargo, the knife upraised. Fargo lowered himself into a crouch, shot his left arm straight upward, and closed his hand around the man's wrist, meeting the downward blow with all the strength in his shoulder muscles. The knife stopped inches away from his face, and the man cursed as he couldn't bring the blade down any further. Fargo was still holding him off when he saw Amity step forward and smash the butt of the carbine into the man's head. The man's arm fell aside and he staggered forward. Fargo, his grip still in place, pitched the man sideways, sending him toppling to the edge of the tent.

He followed through as the man tried to roll away and slash out with the knife all at the same time. Fargo ducked away from the slashing blow, and brought his foot down on the man's forearm. The man cursed in pain as the knife fell from his grip. Fargo bent down, scooped up the hunting knife, and had just brought the blade up in his hand when the man dove at him. In an automatic reaction, Fargo thrust the blade out, and felt it go deep into the man's abdomen. Stepping back, Fargo watched the man pitch forward, both hands clutched to his belly. He collapsed and lay still. Fargo felt Amity beside him. "I just figured out why you stopped me from firing at him," she said.

"Better late than never," he said, then crossed his hands around the man's legs and dragged him from the tent into a thicket of underbrush. "Your hands can get rid of him in the morning," he said to Amity as she stood by the tent.

"How'd you know to come back?" she asked, holding the tent flap open for him to go inside with her.

"Saw him on the hill as I was leaving. Or maybe I should say I smelled him," Fargo said. "I'm thinking the four that tailed you from town weren't just after you for pleasure. Both their horses and his carried the same odor. Coincidence? Damn strange."

"I don't know what to say," Amity answered and lowered herself onto the blanket on her knees. Fargo kneeled down beside her.

"You make any enemies? Anybody that wants to rustle your cattle from you?" he questioned.

Amity thought for a moment. "There were a number of ranchers who were real interested, some very persistent. But there was one, Baxter Carter. I'd have to say I made an enemy of him."

"How?"

"He made me a number of offers that I turned

down. He didn't like taking no for an answer," she said.

"Why'd you turn them down?" Fargo asked.

"I decided he just wanted to make a quick dollar. He wasn't really interested in keeping up the breed and I didn't want to sell to someone like that. He became very angry, even threatened me. I paid no attention to it. Perhaps I should have."

Fargo's lips pursed. "Just because you didn't want to sell to him?"

"There were some other disagreements," she said, suddenly sounding lofty and Fargo half smiled. She wasn't about to give him all the details. That red-headed temper of hers probably played a part in it. It didn't matter that much. She had put Baxter Carter at the top of her list with a belated realization, sobering thoughts shrouding her even-featured face.

"Where is this Baxter Carter?" Fargo asked.

"His place is up by Maple Lake," Amity replied.

Fargo's brow lowered as he thought aloud. "It's on my way to Miles. Maybe I'll pay him a visit," Fargo said.

"Will you come back and tell me what you find? Or decide?" Amity asked.

He tossed her a pained glance. "Not likely. Miles is expecting me and I'm running late as it is now," Fargo said.

"That's not all my doing. You did take your own detours," Amity said.

His shrug was a concession. "I'm here now, though," he said.

Her face softened and she put her hands to his cheeks. "Yes, you are, and I'm grateful for that, for everything you've done. I've no right to ask you to come back. Forget I asked," she said.

"I'll see," he offered and suddenly her lips were on his, no sweet, shy kiss this time but one that was hungering, pressing, urgent. Yet when she pulled away there was embarrassment in her eyes. "You'll have to stop this wrestling with yourself." He smiled.

"It's not easy, dammit, Fargo," she said.

"It won't be, not till you stop," he said. Her mouth came to his again and this time he could feel her breasts' warmth as they pressed into his chest. His hand touched one long curve at the top and she gasped before she pulled away.

"I'm stopping." She hissed, almost angrily, and he laughed as he rose and pulled her to her feet.

"I'm wondering," he said.

"Wondering what?" She glowered.

"Who you're most mad at, yourself or me," he returned.

"You, dammit," she flung back.

"Liar," he said as he ducked from the tent. He heard her muttering angrily as he hurried away, making his way around the edge of the herd and returning to the hill, pausing at the man's horse. Once again, he examined the horse's legs, drew in the dank, pungent odor so he'd lock it inside his memory.

He hurried to where he'd left the Ovaro and rode north over the hill as the first streaks of dawn touched the sky.

5

He paused to sleep a few hours in midmorning, finding a spot under the shade of a basswood, resting beneath the large, heart-shaped leaves until he woke and moved on. He reached Maple Lake in midafternoon. Baxter Carter's spread was easy enough to find, as it was the only cattle ranch in the area. Fargo scanned the terrain as he rode toward the ranch, his practiced eyes taking in the large and the small, from the thick, heavy furrows of hedgerows, stumps, bushes, weeds, grass, and rock to the delicate, tiny white blossoms of the Canada mayflower. He saw the scurry marks where a badger had made its way, the erratic prints of snowshoe rabbits, the sharp, deep marks of white-tailed deer, and he noted the rich soil of no special distinction. He let his nostrils draw in the fresh, clean odor of bluegrass and chamomile.

Nothing dark, dank, or pungent met his nostrils as Baxter Carter's ranch grew larger as he neared it. He passed long, wide corrals that held mostly Herefords with a scattering of Black Angus. His glance moved across long cow barns, bunkhouses, and two stables.

Cowhands paused in their chores as he rode by and drew to a halt outside the main house, a modest yet sturdy structure of red cedar siding and Douglas fir roof shingles. He dismounted and a man opened the door at his knock, a medium-built figure with thick black hair and darting eyes set in a bony face. The man wore an expensive suede shirt of a rusty tan. "Looking for Baxter Carter," Fargo said.

"You found him," the man answered. "Who might you be?"

"Name's Fargo. Come asking about Amity Baker," Fargo said.

"That two-faced little tart," Baxter Carter snapped.

"She didn't have too much good to say about you, either," Fargo said.

"She send you?" the man questioned.

"No. She's been having some trouble. She asked me to get a handle on it," Fargo said evenly.

"Don't come looking here," Baxter Carter growled.

"She said you threatened her," Fargo pushed at him.

Baxter Carter showed no discomfort. "Guess I did. She got me real mad," he said. "She tell you she threatened me with that damned carbine?"

"Don't recall that she did," Fargo said carefully.

"She wouldn't," the man said. "But she did, pointed it right at me. Made me real mad, she did. She agreed to sell me her herd, took a deposit and everything, then changed her damn mind. I made commitments I had to cancel. She refused to give the deposit back, saying it was nonrefundable. Whatever happens to her, it'll be fine with me."

Fargo took in the man's words with more than a little surprise. There was no denial in them, no hiding his feelings, certainly no effort to evade being suspected. His angry frankness was unexpected. Unless he was being especially clever, Fargo pondered, and made note of the thought. "It won't be fine with me," he said.

"You hassling me will bring a lot of trouble, mister, that's for sure," Baxter Carter warned.

"Anything more happens to her will bring a lot more trouble, that's for sure," Fargo said, and turned as the man followed him to the Ovaro. "I'd say we understand each other," Fargo said evenly.

"Reckon so," Carter said, his glower fixed on Fargo as he swung onto the horse and rode from the ranch. Keeping the pinto at a gentle trot, Fargo scanned the ranch buildings again as he went his way, riding into the hackberry, turning through the trees and moving east to the edge of the lake. He dismounted, let the horse drink his fill, and lowered himself to the tall marsh grass at the shore of the lake. His thoughts returned to Baxter Carter again. The man's reaction to Amity's name had been more instant anger than cleverness, spit out without calculation.

But he'd not do any concluding yet, Fargo told himself and he stretched out by the lake and closed his eyes as the day drifted into dusk, the dusk into dark. He let another hour go by before he climbed onto the pinto and began to slowly make his way back to the ranch. When he reached the place he dismounted, left the Ovaro under a tree, and proceeded on foot. A light burned in the main house and another at the far end of the bunkhouse. Everything else was dark. There were no hands outside, and the cattle were in the corrals. Fargo moved on silent steps down the fenceposts around the barns, and slipped into the stable.

He stood very still inside, and let his nostrils pull in scents. The smell of horses came to him, along with the leather of the saddles, hay, and manure, all intertwining to create the very distinctive odor of a stable. He drew in deep breaths again but he smelled nothing more, not the dark, dank, pungent odor he sought to find. Moving forward, he stepped into the first stall, gently ran his hand along the horse's rump, halted, and dropped to one knee. He drew air deeply into his lungs, then took small, sniffing drafts, straightened up, and went into the adjoining stall. He did the same thing there, repeating it in the next stall until he'd gone into each one. Stepping from the last stall, his lips drew back. None of the horses carried even a trace of the acrid, pungent odor. The riders who had attacked Amity hadn't come from these stables or this terrain. These horses smelled only of the distinctive odor of horseflesh. He slid out of the stable and returned to the Ovaro, then walked the horse from the ranch until he was far enough away to take to the saddle in silence.

He rode with thoughts churning inside him. He wouldn't absolutely dismiss Baxter Carter but he'd set him aside as the guilty one for now. Amity had said there were others. Perhaps there were more than she knew about, men who wanted her cattle without her in the way. But he hadn't the time to go chasing down anyone else, Fargo grimaced as he sent the pinto north by west. He'd already delayed too long in getting to Miles Davis. Amity would have to wait. He'd trust her determination and redheaded temper to keep her alive and well.

A day passed before Fargo arrived at the Snake Ditch River, and followed it as it ran alongside the border of the Dakota Territory. He turned east when he reached the Tamarac, staying with the river as it dipped south, and then climbed north until the tall west corner blockhouse of Fort Comber came into sight against a backdrop of black ash and bitternut. From the blockhouse, the stockade of the fort stretched in a large square, its wall of logs pointed at the top with a wood catwalk raised up inside so defenders could fight from a high position. As he neared, Fargo saw it was a sturdy, well-built fort, all its troop quarters and stables contained within its walls. Plenty of embrasures, what most settlers called "shootin' holes," gave the defenders added fire lines. Reaching the fort, Fargo rode inside under the steady gaze of sentries at the open gate and saw that it was, as with most forts, a stopping place for wagon trains and itinerant merchants. A line of eight Conestogas stretched across the inside of the compound, along with produce wagons and closed delivery rigs.

Dismounting, Fargo followed a corporal who took him to the general's quarters. The tall, straight figure rose from behind his desk, silver hair well combed, blue uniform sharply creased as always. But there was none of the dandy about the man. General Miles Davis personified the best about the U.S. Cavalry, an arresting figure who combined dignity with straightforward openness, authority, and understanding. "At last," the general said. "I'm sure glad to see you, Fargo. But then I always am," he added, extending a firm handshake.

"Because you need me or love me?" Fargo laughed.

"Both, old friend," the general returned with his own hearty laugh. "Wish I didn't always have a problem when I call you."

"Wouldn't know what to say if you didn't," Fargo answered. "How long have they had you up here in the north country?"

"Little over a year," the general replied, sliding into his chair. "I'm covering all the way north from the fort and west into the Dakota Territory. The Teton and Santee Dakota and the Pawnee are plenty trouble all through the territory."

Fargo nodded at the general's use of the proper tribal names. To the settlers, the Dakota were all simply Sioux, amongst the fiercest of the plains warriors. "I can see why they sent you," Fargo said.

"At least they gave me a good fort and a crew of experienced cavalry troopers. I'm not the one in trouble," the general said.

"Who is?" Fargo questioned.

"Captain Phil Duncan over at Fort Cox."

"Fort Cox?" Fargo frowned. "Is that fort new? Where is it?"

"Yes, it's northeast, above the Upper Red Lake going toward the South Branch Rapid. It's a piece of garbage tossed together because some senator wanted to put a backer's name on a fort. You know how the army bends in Washington. They stuck it there, figuring it'd just sit harmlessly out of the way. Only, things have suddenly turned out differently."

"How?"

"First, settlers have been streaming down from the border and from Ontario. Now word's reached me that a real Indian uprising is gathering steam, one that's going to explode. So they've got a fort which shouldn't be called a fort with a nice, young officer and an even younger, inexperienced outfit of troops and none of them know a damn thing about Indian fighting, but they're sitting on a volcano."

Fargo let his thoughts reach backward. "The army's done that before," he said.

"And a lot of people have been killed because of it," the general returned and Fargo nodded grimly at words that were all-too true. "As what usually happens, a whole community of settlers have put down roots in the region because of the fort and the troops. They're not aware of the facts, that the troops don't know shit about Indian fighting and the fort isn't worth its name. They're counting on protection from troops that don't know how to protect. They don't realize what the increase in hostile activity really means. A massacre is getting ready to happen up there, Fargo. That's why I called you."

"Not just to have me listen to your story?" Fargo said, sending the general a suspicious glance.

Miles Davis offered a wry smile. "We've come to know each other too well," he said and Fargo grunted in agreement. "You're the only one I can turn to, old friend," the general said.

"Why don't you send them support?" Fargo inquired.

"Hell, I would if I could," the general said and Fargo's eyes questioned. "I've barely enough men to cover my own territory. If I sent even one platoon to Phil Duncan it'd weaken this post. That'd mean my career but, more importantly, it'd jeopardize this entire region. It'd make two commands, neither with enough power to do their job."

"You try getting word to headquarters back East?" Fargo asked.

"Yes, and they turned me down. It seems they're sending every available squad down south because of all this talk about trouble between the states. Besides, the top brass never wanted Fort Cox. Washington politics created it, made the army establish it to stroke some senator's ego or please a big-money supporter. You know what that means, Fargo."

"Yes, they don't give a tinker's damn what happens to the place or anybody in it. Hardly a commendable attitude," Fargo said.

"You're right, not commendable, not justifiable, just reality, the name of the game. Hell, you know that, Fargo," Miles said. "And you know I don't play that way."

"Unfortunately, which makes me suspicious. Offense intended," Fargo said dryly.

"Translation: what do I expect of you?" Miles laughed.

"Bull's-eye," Fargo said.

"I want you to go to Fort Cox. Duncan and his troopers are lost sheep out there, Fargo. Word has reached me that they're even losing sentries and you know what that means."

"It means they don't know how to use sentries properly in Indian country," Fargo said.

"Right, or anywhere else," the general said. "I know the captain. Phil Duncan's young and inexperienced but he's no West Point pompous ass. He'll listen to you. I want you to teach him and his men whatever you can."

"You're joking. You expect I can turn them into experienced Indian fighters overnight?" Fargo asked incredulously.

"No, I'm too much of a realist to expect that. I just want you to teach them enough so that they'll have half a chance, and they won't be complete sitting ducks," the general said.

Fargo continued to stare incredulously. "That might just be impossible to do," he said.

"It might," Miles Davis agreed.

"Or it might already be too late," Fargo said.

"It might," Miles agreed again. "But we'll have tried. That counts."

"For what? Conscience?"

"For maybe one life saved. I'll settle for that," Miles said. "So will you."

Fargo shot him a baleful glance as Miles Davis's words echoed inside him: *We've come to know each other too well.* Words that were too true. "My horse needs a good rubdown and a night's rest. And I need a good meal," he said truculently.

Miles Davis let a broad smile march across his face. "Both coming up," he said.

"Where are you getting your information?" Fargo queried.

"I'll tell you that over dinner," the general said and hurried from the office. Fargo stretched out his long frame in the chair and when Miles Davis returned he was carrying a bottle of bourbon. They shared a toast and then another as talk of old times flowed, memories of yesterdays and problems they had solved together. The company cook brought an excellent meal and by the time it was finished, the general had completed a letter, which he handed to Fargo. "This will explain you and everything else to the captain. It's also a letter formally commissioning you as a citizen operative for the army. It's for Phil Duncan's protection. Anybody quarrels with him later, he can show them that he was acting under my orders. You know the army and protocol."

Fargo sniffed disdainfully. "More than I want to," he said.

"Phil Duncan is a smart-enough officer to know what he doesn't know. But he's also young enough to be unsure of himself, uncertain of what the things going on really mean. He'll welcome any help he can get. He'll introduce you to Joe Beaverhat."

"He your source of information?" Fargo questioned.

"Yes, he got word to me through a traveling drummer," the general said.

"He an army scout?" Fargo asked.

"A good one. I've used him in the past," the general said. "His father was Crow, his mother a half-breed—white and Ojibwa. Joe will give you all the details."

Fargo gave back a sidelong glance. "Smells to me as

if Captain Duncan isn't listening to Joe Beaverhat," he ventured.

"You're right. Phil Duncan's never dealt with an army scout before. I'm sure he doesn't know how much to trust in what Joe Beaverhat's telling him, but you will," Miles said.

Fargo nodded, stuffed the letter into his pocket, and rose. He was shown to a small, neat guest quarters room with a firm cot. He fell asleep quickly and when morning came he found Amity intruding into his thoughts as he remembered where she'd told him she had to deliver the herd: Royce Cantwell's spread near the Moose River. That was squarely in the middle of the region that spread out from Fort Cox, the area Miles had called a volcano.

Fargo grimaced at the thought and let himself hope she'd take enough wrong turns and make enough trail errors to slow her down. Maybe he'd have time to put a lid on the volcano before it erupted. Maybe he wouldn't be able to break trail for her, but maybe he'd get another way to do right by her. When he went outside, Miles was waiting with the Ovaro, the horse all groomed and glistening. "Wish I felt as good as he looks," Fargo muttered.

"I know you'll do your best. That's all I can ask," the general said and he and Fargo exchanged hand clasps. Fargo then pulled himself onto the pinto and rode from the compound. Outside the tall gates, he sent the horse east, and quickly found himself riding through rich terrain. Open land and forests of red ash, bitternut, black walnut, and ironwood competed for space, each adding to the beauty of the other. He made a wide circle north, crossing above Thief Lake. He thought about Royce Cantwell as he continued east. He didn't have the time to pay the man a visit, and there was no reason for it anyway. Amity would be doing that in time. Riding on, Fargo kept a steady pace as he crossed open land, gently rolling hills with glistening lakes looking like so many blue sequins on a vast, green dress. But as he rode, Fargo's continuously searching gaze began to pick up signs that made his lips pull back tightly.

The unshod pony prints were first, many of them appearing in clusters of ten to twelve riders, the perfect number for small, roving hunting parties. Then he paused as he came upon a long line of prints that ran from west to east and finally curved north of the South Branch Rapid. This was no hunting party, but riders on their way somewhere, keeping a neat double line. At least fifty, he estimated. Fargo went straight on as the line of prints climbed north, and it was a half-dozen miles later on that he came to the charred remains of two Conestogas. He halted, surveying the scene. Nothing needed burying but death had struck here, he knew. He counted the unshod prints of one of the smaller hunting parties. Cursing silently, he rode on, eventually coming to a forest of young red ash, where there was plenty of open land between trees.

He weaved his way through the trees and had gone more than halfway through the woods when he heard the high-pitched, sharp, whooping shouts, a sound he knew only too well, a sound that meant only one thing. He put the pinto into a canter, swerving between trees as the shouts grew louder near the end of the woods. He glimpsed a few hundred yards of open land beyond the trees and he slowed the horse, reining it to a halt a few dozen feet from the last line of trees. Staring out at the open land, he saw some thirty near-naked braves on their ponies charging at a row of saplings at the opposite edge of the open land. As he watched, half of them charged on ahead of the others, letting a volley of arrows fly at the line of saplings, and then peeling off into two groups, one swerving right, the other left. Instantly, the next fifteen braves charged the saplings, also sending a fusillade of arrows into the trees. The moment the arrows left their bows, they, too, peeled off into two groups.

As they did, the first fifteen had gathered and were again charging at the saplings, firing off another volley of arrows before again peeling off in two groups. Fargo dropped from the saddle and moved closer to the last of the red ash to peer into the opposite bank of trees. His brow deep with furrows, he stared at the saplings, trying to see figures behind the trees. But he couldn't discern anything, no movement of any kind. The furrows dug deeper into his brow as he saw the braves turn and fire another volley of arrows into the trees. Fargo now saw that the arrows that struck the saplings were not real arrows at all. They were thin shafts of wood without arrowheads, cut in length and thinness to double as arrows.

He continued to stare as the picture changed before his eyes. From something strange and incomprehensible, it suddenly took on a new meaning, a very different and chilling meaning. No one was trapped in the trees. The Indians were not attacking—they were practicing, rehearsing. They were going through maneuvers, staging a mock attack, the makeshift arrows now entirely explainable. Real arrows were not made overnight. They took time and work, and were too valuable to expend shooting at trees. Fargo's eyes went to the line of saplings and they, too, took on a new identity, no longer a row of trees but the sides of a stockade. His eyes were still fastened to the scene before him when another line of riders appeared, racing their ponies close against the saplings as, with one hand, each tossed a bundle of twigs high into the trees.

Fargo watched them retrieve the twigs and repeat the maneuver. His lips pulled back in a grimace as he realized that in a real attack, the bunches of twigs would be lighted bundles of dry grass, used to toss over the stockade wall. He was still watching as the mock attack finally broke off and the riders slowed their ponies, and began to drift away. The sounds of their war whoops came to an end just as his ears caught the soft sound at his back. He turned and saw a branch being brushed back just as the near-naked figure dived at him, tomahawk in hand. Only Fargo's superb reflexes let him pull his head to the side in time to avoid the edge of the tomahawk as it plunged downward, scraping his ear and slamming into the ground.

The Indian pulled the short-handled ax free to strike again, but Fargo brought his knee up and sank it into the man's groin. The Indian let out a grunt of pain as he fell back for a moment, giving enough time for Fargo to swing a short, hard left hook. It caught the man alongside the head and he fell sideways. Fargo rolled and leaped up to charge, but had to dive away as his attacker brought the tomahawk around in a short, vicious arc. Fargo leaped backward as the Indian charged, again his tomahawk raised to rain down another blow. Fargo made no attempt to reach for the Colt. The combat would be fought in silence. A shot would only bring the others with only one result, he realized: his capture, torture, or death.

Fargo's eyes flicked to the man's feet, and saw the Indian's left moccasined foot turn and dig into the ground. A red man had once taught him the trick of watching your opponent's feet, and Fargo was ready for the tomahawk's trajectory as the ax came in from the left. His hand shot up and closed around the Indian's wrist, the tomahawk now hung suspended in midair inches from his face. With his right fist, Fargo sank a powerhouse blow deep into the man's abdomen. The Indian gasped out, his face contorting in pain, his strength deserting him for the moment. Fargo twisted the man's wrist hard, and the tomahawk dropped from his hand. Releasing his hold on the man's wrist, he bent down and scooped up the weapon. He then looked up to see the Indian had recovered enough strength to dive at him, both hands outstretched to encircle his neck.

Fargo brought the tomahawk in his hand up in a short uppercut of a blow, as much in defense as anything else. The ax and the man's chin met in midair, and Fargo grimaced as he heard the splintering of bone. He rolled clear as his attacker pitched facedown on the ground, his head all but split in half. Fargo drew a deep breath as he pushed to his feet. He glanced through the trees. The riders were leaving, circling around the line of saplings. They had heard nothing. Their practice session was now at an end. He watched them disappear from sight and brought his eyes back to the figure at his feet.

A snare hung from the Indian's waistband. He'd been out hunting small game; rabbits, probably. If he was part of the ones practicing for war, they wouldn't miss him for hours. Fargo's eyes paused on the armband around the man's upper arm, then went to his moccasins. Both were covered with tribal decorations and Fargo's brow furrowed again as he took in the symmetrical quill work with the beaded borders. "Yankton Dakota," he muttered aloud, disbelief in his voice. "This far east?" he asked. He glanced down at the figure again as the words rolled through his mind. Was the man a renegade, a loner far from his people? Fargo considered the question. The explanation was entirely possible, and also entirely too coincidental. But he decided to embrace the explanation for now.

Fargo swung onto the Ovaro, crossed the open space, and went into the trees behind the row of saplings as he rode east. But the markings on the Indian stayed in his mind as he rode, like an unwelcome and ominous passenger.

6

The afternoon had begun to lengthen when Fargo saw the river appear at his left. He had already passed another burned wagon before he swung closer to ride parallel to the river. Soon after he began to see signs that he was on the right trail to the fort. Wagon tracks came into view, first the deep treadmarks of heavy Conestogas, then the lighter ones of farm wagons and the occasional thin treads of a buckboard. A house appeared soon after, a small farm with four little boys methodically tossing shelled corn into furrowed rows of good, rich soil. Other houses came into sight as he rode at a slow, steady pace. Two young girls, perhaps fifteen or so, fed ears of corn to a dozen Tamworth hogs.

Three larger farms were next, with many varieties of vegetables growing in the plowed fields. Fargo glimpsed squash, turnips, cabbages, beets, and melons. The houses were all newly built, their saddle-notched logs hardly weathered. None had a root cellar or stone storehouse where refuge could be taken, he noted. It was plain they all trusted the protection of the army, despite the increase in Indian activity. The ordinary traveler would see only the face of a peaceful land, but Fargo was no ordinary traveler. He rode a winding pattern and saw a number of Indian pony prints that crisscrossed the land, most of them coming from the north. Some were lone riders, others roaming bands. When he found a torn anklet in a clump of grass he halted and studied the beadwork, decided it was probably Winnebago, and rode on with a frown creasing his brow.

The day was ending when he saw the fort, set back about a thousand yards from the river. He didn't turn toward it, but purposely kept to a path that let him appear to be but a passing rider. But Fargo's lake blue eyes narrowed as he peered at the fort, studying it closely. He saw that the land around it had been cleared away, but not far enough. Heavy stands of hackberry and black ash rose up only a few hundred yards from the cleared area. As he surveyed the fort, everything Miles Davis had said was all too true. Fort Cox was a hastily erected excuse for a proper fort. There were no corner blockhouses, and sentries were stationed atop the catwalks behind the top of the stockade walls. The gates of the compound were loosely hinged, and there were no embrasures cut into the stockade walls to allow defenders to fire from a protected position. Even the stockade walls were thinly caulked.

More disturbingly, Fargo saw at least two dozen families that had set up outside the side walls of the fort. Some were plainly marking time before going on to carve their homesteads out in the wilderness, but others seemed to have settled in to live within the fort's shadow and sold garments and home-fashioned cook utensils to the garrison. They were too close to the fort, their presence a distraction and a potential problem. A properly run fort would not have permitted them to camp under its nose. Fargo was still scanning the tents when a platoon of troopers arrived and walked their horses into the fort.

He watched them go by and grimaced inwardly as he saw only young, earnest, unlined faces as they disappeared into the compound. Darkness descended as outside lamps were lighted in the compound. Cooking fires began to flicker in front of some of the tents. But still, Fargo didn't turn and ride into the fort. Instead, he rode on his way, past the cleared area and into the stand of hackberry where he retraced his steps until he could look out at the entire front line of the fort. Something Miles Davis had said swam into his mind. He could have his meeting with Captain Duncan in the morning, Fargo decided. Meanwhile, there was nothing more dramatically effective than an object lesson. Maybe he'd have the chance to give one, and save a life at the same time, Fargo told himself. He had nothing to lose, he decided, and lowered himself against a tree trunk and closed his eyes. He'd catnap, take in a few hours of sleep, and bide his time before putting his plan into effect. The small, steady sounds from the fort and the tents surrounding it drifted to him, soft murmurings, the scrape of pots and pans, and the slap of leather and harness from inside the compound.

They were, in their own way, soothing, reassuring sounds that filtered dimly into his half sleep. He didn't know how long it had been, two maybe three hours, he guessed, when he snapped awake. The sounds had ended. The silence woke him as if it had been a bugle. He leaned forward, and peered through the moonlight to the fort, seeing that the gate was closed. The distant snort of a horse echoed from inside the compound and the line of tents outside the side wall were dark and still. Fargo took note of two sentries slowly walking the high catwalk that looked over the stockade wall. He also saw four sentries on foot outside the fort, one at each corner of the front of the stockade, one posted at each side of the fort.

They were stationary, each man's gaze focused on the trees beyond the cleared land, as were the sentries patrolling along the catwalk. Fargo peered at each of the sentries, tracing a line from each man out across the open ground. As his eyes moved back and forth from sentry to sentry, he saw they were all focusing on the trees and a grim smile edged his lips. His own eyes continued to glare from sentry to sentry and across the open land in front of each man. Perhaps another hour had passed when Fargo caught a movement on the ground near the sentry standing guard in front of the tents. His eyes peered at the form on the ground, saw the furred back of a coyote, the white markings along the sides standing out against the dark ground. His eyes stayed on the furry form, seeing it move closer to the sentry. Fargo's eyes narrowed. The animal went forward in short, quick bursts of movement and

Fargo smiled. This was no coyote, he thought. A coyote would move forward at a slow, half crawl, carefully edging its way forward.

Fargo rose, drew the double-edged blade from the calf holster at his leg, dropped into his own crouch, and stayed in the trees until he was opposite the sentry, directly behind the furry object. His eyes flicked to the sentry. The man's eyes were focused on the trees as Fargo crept into the open, dropping to his stomach and pushing himself forward. He crept up directly behind the animal, halted, then raised his arm. The thin throwing knife sailed through the air. Fargo saw it hurtle into the furred back in front of him and while Fargo watched, the form shuddered, crawled a few inches, shuddered again, then lay still.

Fargo's eyes cut to the sentry. The man continued to gaze toward the treeline not noticing any movement before him. Fargo glanced at the next nearest sentry. The man's eyes were completely concentrated on the distant trees as well. Fargo gathered himself, and rose. With a burst of movement driven by his powerful legs, he was at the sentry in front of him in a second, the Colt pressed into the man's side. The sentry's eyes widened in complete surprise. "Don't move. Drop the rifle," Fargo hissed, and the man obeyed. "Now, if I were an Indian, your throat would be cut by now and I might be dragging you into the trees," Fargo whispered.

The man swallowed hard. "Jesus, who are you?" he managed.

"A guardian angel," Fargo said, keeping his gun

into the man's ribs. "Start walking to the gate." Fargo stayed against him as the sentry started toward the gate. The nearest sentry saw him and turned, stared.

"Jerry? What the hell is this?" the sentry called.

"Get the gate," Fargo answered.

"Do what he says," the sentry added. "He's crazy." The second sentry backed up, reached the gate, and pounded on it. A trooper appeared inside, and opened a door cut into the main gate as Fargo pushed the young man inside in front of him.

"Get Captain Duncan," Fargo ordered. The trooper turned and ran to a small structure, a company flag hanging beside the door. He returned in moments with a young man still slipping on his uniform jacket. Fargo saw his earnest face, and the short blond mustache that echoed his blond hair.

"What the hell's going on here?" the captain barked.

Still keeping the Colt into the sentry's ribs, Fargo handed the captain General Davis's letter. The trooper standing beside him picked up a lamp and held it up for the captain to read. When he finished reading, the captain looked up at Fargo. "All right, General Davis sent you. Did he tell you to come in here and scare one of my sentries half to death?" The captain scowled.

"No, that was my idea," Fargo replied.

The captain's brow lifted. "May I ask why?" he returned with an edge in his voice.

"It's called an object lesson. You won't forget what's happened here tonight, none of you will," Fargo said, seeing another uniformed figure step closer, a lieutenant's bars on his jacket.

"Lieutenant Jones, my second in command," Captain Duncan said.

Fargo nodded curtly. "Your man would be dead now if I hadn't been waiting and watching in the trees," Fargo said and drew the gun from the sentry's ribs. "You'll find a coyote skin outside," he added.

"The coyote?" the sentry blurted. "I saw him. They're always sneaking around. I didn't pay any mind to him."

"You'll find a dead brave under the coyote fur. He was on his way to kill you," Fargo said, and saw the young man's face turn a shade whiter.

"Go look. Take Anderson with you," the captain said and the sentry hurried away with another trooper.

"Bring back my throwing knife," Fargo called after him.

"Please come inside," Captain Duncan said, motioning to the lieutenant. "You, too, Ralph." Fargo followed both men into a small office. A territory map hung on one wall and two straight-backed chairs faced a wooden desk. Duncan handed the lieutenant the letter and when he finished reading it, the officer glanced up at Fargo.

"You sure know how to get a man's attention, Fargo," Lieutenant Jones said wryly.

"Nothing like a good entrance," Fargo said as he lowered himself into one of the chairs. Captain Duncan's eyes were fastened on the Trailsman as he took the letter back from the lieutenant.

"This letter leaves a lot unsaid, Fargo," the captain noted just as the door opened and the trooper returned, handing Fargo the thin-bladed knife, awe still wreathing his young face.

"He was right, sir," the sentry said, turning to the captain. "There's an Indian under a coyote skin out there."

"Thank you, trooper. Dismissed," the captain said curtly and eased himself into a chair behind the desk once the trooper left. "Object lesson duly noted, Fargo," he said. "I'm sure you've already surmised that wouldn't have been the first sentry we've lost."

"So I heard," Fargo said.

"It's been increasing. Obviously, we're doing something wrong," the captain said.

"Yes, putting sentries out to watch for Indian attacks isn't just putting out sentries. The Indian can outdo a fox in cunning and stealthiness," Fargo said. "Why are you putting sentries out beyond the fort's walls?"

"To protect the families living in those tents. We could bring them inside the fort every night, but it'd be awkward."

"It'd also give the impression that you're afraid, and you don't want that. You want to show you can hold your ground and fight back and win," Fargo surmised. "That means you need to have sentries watching sentries. One group of sentries you put outside to watch the trees, as they're doing now. Other sentries on the wall could watch over them and shoot anything that moves near."

Captain Duncan nodded, and glanced over at the lieutenant. "Put that into operation tomorrow," he said, then glanced at the letter still in his hands. "I'm grateful General Davis sent you but is he sending me another message? Is he telling me not to expect any more troops?"

"Go to the head of the class," Fargo said. "Now, tell me what you know about the attacks."

"Only that they've been steadily increasing. As you saw, they've taken to killing my sentries, and my patrols are coming under attack more often, but I don't really know what it all means," Phil Duncan said.

"The attacks on the sentries and on your patrols are easy enough to figure. They're testing, probing, feeling you out," Fargo said.

"What do they expect to find out?" the lieutenant asked.

"Sporadic attacks on your sentries will tell them how good your defenses are at the fort. The attacks on your patrols are designed to tell them how good your troops are at their kind of fighting. But it's still all just a test. The question remains, what does it mean," Fargo said.

"I wish I knew. I think they're just acting up, a passing attempt at making themselves feel big. The Winnebago have been quiet for a long while. So have the Ojibwa and the Saux-Fox. I think they're just showing off. They're not really up to anything more," the captain said.

"General Davis thinks you're sitting on a volcano. Is he right?"

"Joe Beaverhat thinks that, too," the captain said. "I'd guess he got the word to the general."

"You don't agree?" Fargo asked. "Why are you holding back?"

Phil Duncan had the honesty to look uncomfortable. "I don't know how much to believe Joe Beaverhat. I don't understand the Indian ways, I'll admit that. I didn't know if he's exaggerating. He may be a good scout but does he have good judgment? He says things but doesn't give me any reasons. He just says he knows and I ought to take his word."

Fargo allowed a wry smile as he appreciated Phil Duncan's straightforward manner. "That's not unusual for the Indian. They're not big on trying to convince you. They speak their piece and leave it there. I want to talk to him."

"He has a lean-to north of here by Pebble Lake. I can take you there in the morning," the lieutenant put in.

"Good. Meanwhile, you can carry on as usual for the rest of the night. There won't be any other attempts on your sentries," Fargo said.

"I'll show you to the guest quarters and have your horse stabled," Jones added.

"He's tethered by the ash opposite the fort gate," Fargo said, and followed the lieutenant to a neatly furnished guest quarters, where he quickly undressed and stretched out on the cot. Phil Duncan had been honest in admitting his inability to evaluate Joe Beaverhat and the overall threat. He'd listen, not let ego get in the way. That was the only good thing. Everything else, from the mock attack he'd watched, to the attempt on the sentry by the Yankton Dakota brave left Fargo with a feeling of foreboding. He knew it was not something he'd be shaking off easily, and he went to sleep wrapped up with the thought, an irritating, uncomfortable blanket.

The bugle sounding reveille woke him in the morning, and when he finished dressing, he went outside to find the Ovaro waiting along with Lieutenant Jones mounted on a sturdy standard army dark bay. With the lieutenant leading the way, Fargo rode due north over low hills, open land, and forests of red maple. Finally, an irregularly shaped lake appeared directly in front of him and the lieutenant halted at the water's edge. "We wait. Joe Beaverhat will find us." It didn't take long before the Indian scout appeared, stepping out from the trees. Fargo saw he was of medium build, wearing elkskin trousers, a cartridge belt across his chest, and a white, sleeveless shirt open in front. A pistol hung in the holster at his waist. Fargo saw how he got his call name—a battered beaver hat sat atop his head as though it had grown there, giving him an air of incongruous dignity.

His face, reddish brown in skin color, was of typical broad-cheeked Indian visage but without any tribal markings. Only his eyes, a smoky blue, betrayed the white blood in him. Lieutenant Jones saluted and the scout raised one palm. "Somebody to see you," Jones said. "He is called Fargo. General Davis sent him." Fargo saw an expression flicker across Joe Beaverhat's impassive face. The lieutenant, in a gesture of courtesy and diplomacy that impressed Fargo, moved a dozen yards away.

Fargo let the scout's eyes take him in for a moment

before he spoke. "General Davis told me to find you, to listen to you," Fargo said.

"General Davis good man," Joe Beaverhat said, his face losing some of its impassivity.

"General Davis sent me to show soldiers how to fight with Indian," Fargo said.

The scout made a derisive sound that Fargo let pass. "I have seen things, not good things. I saw a Yankton Dakota out here," Fargo said.

"You see plenty more," the scout said.

"Why?" Fargo frowned.

"Winnebago, Saux-Fox, Kickapoo, Ojibwa, all want to drive out settlers and soldiers," Joe Beaverhat said.

"They tried that once before and lost," Fargo reminded him.

"Since that time they are like fire that will not go out," the scout replied, the metaphor both simple and profound, painting a picture of anger and pride that still burned.

"What makes them think they can win this time?" Fargo asked.

"They look into themselves, learn that they are not fierce warriors like plains tribes, like Cheyenne, Arapaho, Crow, Comanche, Dakotas. This time they go to Yankton Dakota, make blood pact to share all land for their help to drive out settlers and horse soldiers."

Fargo turned the scout's words over in his mind. It would be a blood pact, all right, sealed with the blood of countless men, women, and children. For the Winnebago and the others, it would restore pride. For the Dakotas, it would give them land they never had.

"How many of the Dakotas have come here?" he asked. "How many with the Winnebago, Saux-Fox, and the others?"

"Two hundred, maybe more," Joe Beaverhat said after a moment's thought.

Fargo cursed under his breath. He hadn't seen the full complement of the fort but he doubted that Phil Duncan had much over a hundred troopers at his command, maybe one hundred and twenty-five if he put cooks, carpenters, and stableboys into the saddle. Joe Beaverhat's estimate echoed ominously. "Two hundred, maybe more, huh," Fargo muttered. "Who leads them?"

"Chief Otaktay," the scout said and Fargo winced at the name.

"How does Joe Beaverhat know all this?" Fargo asked.

"I watch, I listen, I learn," the scout said.

"They have a camp?" Fargo asked.

"Big war camp, with women to cook."

"Can you take me there?" Fargo asked and saw a hint of fear in the scout's impassive face.

"You want to get yourself killed?" Joe Beaverhat said.

"I want to see the camp for myself. I want to see how many Dakota are there. I want to see everything about camp," Fargo said.

A grunt laced with understanding came from the scout's broad-cheeked face. "No good. Captain Duncan not strong enough to attack camp," the scout said.

"I'm sure you're right. I still want to see," Fargo insisted.

"I take you close, only close, no more," the scout said.

"Good enough. Later today. I'll come back," Fargo said and the man nodded, watching Fargo walk to where the lieutenant waited respectfully.

"The captain's taking out the morning patrol. We can meet him. He'll be going our usual way," Lieutenant Jones said.

"What's that?"

"A series of long circles that lets us check out every one of the settlers' camps," Lieutenant Jones said.

"Let's go," Fargo said. His face stayed grim as he rode with the lieutenant across a low hill, onto a wide path where tall ironwoods lined one side. Red ash grew where the land dipped on the other side. "Are your squads always attacked at the same spot?"

"No. They hit us at different places," Jones said.

"I'd expect so," Fargo muttered just as he saw the patrol approaching, the captain heading the column of twos. He counted twenty troopers and nodded in satisfaction. Phil Duncan was enough of a tactician not to send out a weak force.

"Learn anything from Joe Beaverhat?" the captain asked as Fargo swung in beside him.

"The general's right about the volcano," Fargo said. "You're not dealing with just the Winnebago, the Saux-Fox, and the Ojibwa. They've brought in the Yankton Dakota." Phil Duncan's eyes grew wide. "Exactly. That's another breed of polecat. The chief leading them is called Otaktay. You know what that name means?" Fargo queried.

"No," Duncan said.

"It means One Who Kills Many," Fargo said. "He's real bad medicine."

"Jesus," the captain murmured.

"It gets worse. With the Winnebago, Kickapoo, Ojibwa, and Saux-Fox, they'll outnumber you at least two to one. But it'll be the Yankton Dakota that will be the most deadly. You can count on that."

"You paint a pretty bad picture, Fargo," Phil Duncan said. "You sound like throwing in the towel is the only answer, but you know we can't do that. That's not the army way."

"The Dakota wouldn't let you, anyway," Fargo said.

"We just prepare and hope we can win?" the lieutenant asked. "We just sit back and wait? I'd rather attack than that."

"Attacking might just get everybody killed faster," the captain replied.

"I just got here. I want to do my own probing. I might just find a weak spot we can use," Fargo said. "Meanwhile, I'll be trying to forge your men into Indian fighters."

"We'll do anything we can to help, Fargo," the captain said.

"Let's start with your routine patrol," Fargo said, and the captain nodded and ordered the platoon forward. Fargo dropped a few paces behind him as the patrol turned onto another side road. Fargo saw a line of six houses appear. The captain swung closer to them, and as the platoon rode by, figures waved back at them. Turning onto a wide deer trail, Captain Duncan led the way past a thin line of alders. Fargo's eyes swept the terrain, roaming across a hill on his right that was well grown with bitternut. His eyes never stopped scanning the land on both sides of the trail, and soon they passed another cluster of four settlements. Leaving the settlers behind, the captain made a long, slow turn alongside the low hills when Fargo moved up alongside him.

"You know we've had company for the last three miles," Fargo said calmly.

Phil Duncan's eyes widened in surprise. He pulled his eyes from Fargo, let them dart away, first to one side of the road, then the trees at the other side. "I don't see anything," Duncan said.

"One brave in the trees. He's gone now, went on ahead," Fargo said.

"I suppose that's to be expected, their watching us, no?"

"That's right. Only from now on, you'll have two men riding lookout on every patrol. I want you watching them watching you," Fargo said.

"Make a note of that," Duncan tossed to the lieutenant as they rode on. The patrol rode on and a curve in the wide trail came into sight just as shots rang out from beyond the turn. The captain sent his patrol into an instant gallop and Fargo stayed right behind him. When they rounded the curve, Fargo saw the land dip down to where some ten braves were racing around two Conestogas, three of the Indians pouring rifle fire into the wagons. A line of alder rose up just in back of the two Conestogas, and Fargo's eyes narrowed as he swept the scene from back to front. "Charge!" he heard the captain's shouted command.

"No," Fargo snapped out and the captain reined up, held up one hand, and stared at him.

"What's the matter with you? People are being attacked down there," the captain threw at him.

"Send half the squad. Hold the rest here," Fargo said.

Still frowning in confusion, Duncan barked orders. "First ten troopers charge," he said. Fargo saw the riders streak past him on their way down to the wagons, his eyes riveted on the braves racing around the wagons. "Why only half?" he heard the captain ask.

"We'll play their game," Fargo said, his eyes on the scene below as the troopers charged the circling braves. The Indians broke off their attack at once, and started to race away as the troopers charged after them. Fargo's eyes were already on the end of the tree line when a second, larger group of near-naked figures charged out, bearing down on the troopers from the side. Fargo saw the troopers, taken completely by surprise, rein up and try to circle away from the new force of attackers. He saw two clutch at their arms as rifle fire erupted from the second group of Indians. "*Now!*" Fargo yelled and sent the Ovaro downhill, hearing the remainder of the troop thundering after him. The captain hurtled past him, his men in a full charge, firing as they struck the second knot of Indians from behind.

Fargo saw the braves turn in surprise, two toppling

from their ponies. They made little effort to fight back and turned, beginning to streak away. Being taken by surprise invariably rattled Indian fighters, their answer was usually to retreat, rather than stay for any further surprises. As they raced away, Captain Duncan shouted a halt to his men. Fargo reached them as they reined up and began to turn to the wagons. "See to the people in there. They may be alive," the captain told Lieutenant Jones.

"Don't bother," Fargo said and Duncan's eyes turned to him, consternation again flooding his young face. "There's nobody in those wagons," Fargo said. "They were put here as decoys. It was all a trap, the attack, too, everything designed to bring you charging into their ambush."

"Playing their game," Phil Duncan said, awe and respect in his voice as he stared at Fargo.

"Turning tables." Fargo nodded.

One of the troopers came up from the wagons, and halted before the captain. "They're empty, sir, nobody in them," he said.

"Thank you," Duncan said and turned to Fargo, veneration coloring his voice. "How'd you know?" he asked.

"There was no return fire from the wagons. Indians don't keep firing into wagons when there's no return fire. They don't waste bullets or arrows on dead people. You thought the wagons were firing back because of the show they put on," Fargo said.

"I sure did," Phil Duncan replied.

"To fight the Indian, you have to look before you

leap. You have to learn to see what's really going on, not just what he wants you to see," Fargo said.

"But that takes time and experience," Duncan said.

"This'll be a crash course," Fargo said. "Let's finish the patrol."

The captain nodded and sent his two wounded men back with an escort before continuing the patrol. They rode on slowly, Fargo making mental notes of landmarks and terrain, and the places where settlers had put down roots. Most were clustered in groups of three to six, he noted, more for a sense of neighborhood than protection, he suspected. Yet they might well owe their lives to their neighborly tendencies, he reflected. When the captain turned the patrol to head back to the fort, Fargo slowed as they drew opposite Pebble Lake. "I'm going to do some exploring with Joe Beaverhat," he said.

"We'll have a briefing session for all the men at the fort tonight. They'll learn what you've taught us. We'll drill it in until it's part of them. When will you be back?" the captain asked.

"Maybe tonight, maybe tomorrow. I'll be doing some more intensive training when I do," Fargo said and rode east as the patrol moved on its way to the fort. He'd tried to leave them with both hope and reality. They'd need both to survive, one to sustain the other. Thoughts of surviving brought Amity's carrot-top prettiness to him. Maybe she'd be the lucky one after all, and manage to deliver her herd and get out before all hell broke loose. That finality seemed more and more certain, one more reason why taking in the

Dakota camp was so important. He had to see if it held something he could use. Perhaps his scouting would reveal a flaw, a weakness. His thoughts drifted as he reached Pebble Lake. Joe Beaverhat appeared a few minutes later, sitting atop a short-legged, claybank-colored Indian pony.

Saying nothing, the scout started off, leading Fargo along a thick forest of shrubby alders that finally came to an end, leaving only open land stretching beyond. "I stop here," Joe Beaverhat said. "Army not pay me enough to kill myself. Dakota camp straight ahead, mile, maybe."

"All open land?" Fargo asked.

"Few trees, not many. Thick fields of what you call milk thistle," the scout said. "You take big chance, Fargo."

"Bad habit of mine," Fargo said. "Talk more when I get back."

"Maybe," Joe Beaverhat said and Fargo, realizing the meaning behind the word, sent the pinto forward. He rode slowly as the last of the alders thinned out. He was soon riding across open land. When he spied a small cluster of quaking aspen, he went into the trees and tied the Ovaro to a branch in the center. He moved out on foot and saw the thick field of milk-thistle, differing from the ordinary thistle by the size of the milky white veins coursing through each long leaf. To Fargo, its appeal wasn't its rose pink flowers but its six-foot height. Dropping to his stomach, he slid his way through the broad, veined leaves.

He crawled his way forward slowly, even though he

was not yet in sight of the camp. He wanted no wandering brave or sharp-eyed squaw to see the movement of the leaves. As he made his way, the camp appeared in front of him. He counted at least twenty teepees with plenty of space between each one, where Indian blankets dotted the ground. Loincloth-clad braves on foot engaged in every sort of activity, from wrapping arrow shafts with strengthening reeds to using wood staves in hand-to-hand combat exercises. Fargo's eyes traveled across the camp as he crawled still closer. He saw a half-dozen cooking fires lighted, bare-breasted women tending to them. He also saw dozens of younger women scattered among the teepees, many more than were needed to skin and cook food, he noted. The chief wanted his warriors satisfied in every way.

His eyes came to a halt along one side of the camp where he saw a half-dozen braves keeping watch over some two dozen open boxes of gleaming rifles that appeared to be .52 caliber Spencers, undoubtedly captured in a raid on an army supply wagon. To Fargo, they meant only one thing. The Dakota would not be relying solely on the accuracy of their arrows. He halted as he realized he was perilously close to the end of the tall milk-thistle, and lay still as his gaze moved to the far end of the camp. The Indian ponies were tethered in long lines of rawhide ropes. He grimly counted them, stopping when he had reached a hundred, and saw as many more on other tethers. He brought his eyes back to the camp as dusk began to settle in. He was still watching when a teepee in the center of the camp became the focus for a dozen braves. He followed their gaze and saw a figure emerge from the tent, tall, well-muscled, wearing a dark blue breechcloth over leggings, a bear-claw necklace hanging against his chest, a single feather in his long black hair, slicked down with fish oil.

Fargo didn't need to hear the braves murmur the man's name as he took in his strong, clean features, the eagle nose and wide cheekbones typical of the Dakota people. "Otaktay," Fargo muttered into the leaves, noting the cruel cast to the man's expression, a look that fitted his name. A glance at the braves giving the chief way showed that they were Ojibwa and Winnebago, the beadwork on their moccasins distinctly the work of those tribes. The chief halted before the boxes of rifles and picked one up to examine it. Fargo saw that it was indeed a .52 caliber Spencer repeating rifle. Otaktay put the rifle down and now a small crowd had gathered around him, most of them Dakota. The chief spoke as others came around to listen. Though the Winnebago, Ojibwa, and Kickapoo spoke Algonquian, they had apparently familiarized themselves enough with the Siouxan language to understand him. Fargo himself knew more than enough Siouxan to understand the chief.

"We must keep doing what we have been doing, keep weakening them, a little here, a little there. When we really attack, they fall as overripe fruit falls from a tree. They will be too weak to save themselves or the others who defile our lands," Otaktay said as a cheer went up from his listeners. Fargo's lips pressed together in a thin line, the Dakota's words a confirmation of what he suspected the Indians were doing. But it reinforced his own decisions, and he let his eyes travel across the camp once more before darkness fell. He made a note of the fact that there were no sentries. The chief had set his camp far enough away from the trees. No force of any size could approach without crossing open land, awaking the camp. Overconfidence could be a weakness. His glance cut to the horses. They were tethered too far behind the edge of the camp, he decided. They couldn't be reached in seconds. Noting the fact, Fargo placed it in his mind alongside the camp's overconfidence.

As night fell, he started to back his way through the tall weeds, forcing himself to move slowly, keeping the stalks of milk-thistle motionless. The light from the cooking fires reached out to where he lay in the tall foliage, so he inched his way until he was beyond the edge of light. Turning, then, he crawled forward and finally reached the aspen where he'd left the Ovaro. He rode from the trees, back along the tree line, letting plans form in his mind. They were uncertain, dubious schemes that gave him little comfort. Yet they were all he had, and he rode with the hope that something better might yet come to him. The night was deep when he reached Pebble Lake, and he was about to go on when he saw the dark shape of a horse and rider standing to one side. He drew closer to see Joe Beaverhat take form in the moonlight.

"You waited," Fargo said. "A compliment or just curiosity?"

"Both," the scout said. "You find anything?"

"Nothing to make me happy. They're preparing. They will attack as soon as they're ready," Fargo said.

"You find something I don't know?" the scout said sharply.

"They're overconfident," Fargo said.

Joe Beaverhat frowned back. "I do not know this word."

Fargo searched for another way to convey the meaning. "They are too happy with themselves," he said, finally.

"Aha," the scout said, nodding in understanding. "But they have good reason," he added.

"I know, dammit," Fargo snapped. "But if I can change things, maybe they'll think twice about attacking. Maybe they'll hold off."

"A river does not change its course," Joe Beaverhat stated and Fargo swore softly at his simple wisdom.

"I just want to buy time," Fargo replied and the scout shrugged. Fargo did not go into his reasons. They were all frail, tenuous. He wanted time to turn Duncan's men into a fighting force. He needed time for Miles Davis to convince headquarters to send reinforcements. And he wanted time to find a way to strike at the Dakota chief. But he held the thoughts inside himself, and turned the pinto to ride on. "I'll come visiting some more," he said to the scout, who nodded back. Fargo rode through the night, and when he reached the fort, the moon hung high in the midnight sky. The guard at the gate admitted him and a trooper took his horse. Fargo went directly to the guest quarters, undressed, and welcomed sleep as it blanketed him, both a comfort and a refuge.

7

The morning brought its own surprise as Fargo went outside to find the captain had assembled the entire company for him. " 'Morning, Fargo," Phil Duncan said brightly. "Figured it'd save time to have everyone listen to you at once."

"The men have been briefed thoroughly about yesterday," Lieutenant Jones said. "Thought you'd like to take it further yourself."

Fargo faced the young faces in neat rows, all eyes on him with a combination of interest and politeness. "I'll be working with each platoon separately. Everything will apply to all of you. Over all, you have to first understand what fighting the Indian means. First and foremost, it means self-discipline. It means holding back, not fighting on his terms. But mostly, it means not letting yourself be tricked. We're going to practice that, starting with the first platoon on patrol."

"I'll take Platoon C on morning patrol," Lieutenant Jones said. "Sergeant Baker will take Platoon D on the afternoon patrol. We'll rotate until every trooper and officer has had a chance to learn what we have to learn. Platoon C, get your mounts. Everyone else, dismissed." As the men went their ways, the lieutenant turned to Fargo. "You'll be riding along, I hope," he said.

"That's right," Fargo said. "First thing is to divide the platoon into two sections. Half will ride point, the other half rides far enough back to be out of sight but still be able to hear the bugler. If you hear the bugle, you come charging." The lieutenant saw to the division of the platoon, twelve men in each group, and in minutes Fargo rode from the fort beside him. The lieutenant took the usual route the patrol covered, and soon they swung by the first set of settlers in their cabins. Fargo uttered a sardonic sound inside himself at the peacefulness of the scene, wondering how long it would last. They had gone but another three miles when the peacefulness was shattered.

The band of loinclothed riders came over the top of a low rise, already in a full gallop, firing both arrows and bullets. Fargo's quick count told him there were at least fifteen warriors. "Spread out! Form a line, leaving plenty of space between you," Fargo said. With the lieutenant leading them, the troopers formed a line. It made them a harder target than if they stayed together, and let them lay down a steady volley.

"Fire!" Lieutenant Jones shouted and the troopers exploded a fusillade of lead from their horses. As he expected, it took only moments for the Indians to wheel around and race away. "No pursuit," the lieutenant called out.

"Good. You're a quick study." Fargo smiled, his eyes

on the cluster of Indian ponies. He saw them rein to a halt, realizing they weren't being chased. They milled for a moment, gathering themselves, as one brave made a pumping motion with one arm. A nearby line of red maple spewed forth another dozen riders. They joined the first group and began to charge forward. "Bugler!" Fargo called out, and the sound of the horn instantly sliced through the air. The backup half of the patrol raced up just as the Dakota charged forward in a column of two. As the troop fired a dense volley of bullets from their central, concentrated position, the first half of the patrol kept its line and poured gunfire into the attackers from both ends.

Fargo saw at least six of the Dakota go down, the others drawing up, taken by surprise by being hit hard by the double-pronged firepower. Fargo saw another two toppled from their ponies before they turned. Again, the lieutenant called back any pursuit and Fargo's eyes stayed on the Dakota, watched them keep riding away until they disappeared over another low rise. "They're finished. They won't be coming back to attack again. They'll be reporting this back at the camp," Fargo said as the platoon gathered around. He took the troopers in with a sweeping glance. "You did well. This is what you'll do from now on, with every patrol that's attacked. And they'll attack again, another patrol, another place, another time. But you hold to what you did here today. Once they decide they can't trick you, and sucker you into ambushes, they'll back off."

"Lesson understood and noted," the lieutenant said

to Fargo. "We'll go on and complete our patrol rounds."

"I'll see you later, tonight, probably," Fargo said, stood back, and watched the lieutenant ride off with his patrol in two sections. Fargo allowed himself a feeling of satisfaction as the troop went on its way. It had gone well. They were learning what it meant to fight the Indian. Of course, there was still a lot more to learn. That's why buying time was so important. But he knew he couldn't count on buying a lot. There were other parts of the picture he had to explore. When you sat on a volcano, you had to prepare for the worst. He sent the pinto across open land to the west and began to make his own rounds of the small clusters of settlements that dotted the land. He paused to exchange pleasantries with a number of them, then came to a halt at a small farm run by a spare-framed man and his wife, along with their two teenage daughters. "Ned Calligan and Sarah," the man introduced. "And this here's Jessie and Jessica."

They became even friendlier when he told them he was on a special assignment for Captain Duncan. He agreed to their invitation to stay for dinner as the dusk began to descend, seeing an opportunity he wanted to gauge the settlers' mindframe while having some polite conversation. "You think the settlers would stay at the fort if the army asked them to?" he probed after a dessert of freshly baked apple pie. "Say the captain had word of an Indian uprising."

"You mean leave their homes, everything they've

built to be burned down by the Indians?" Ned Calligan questioned.

"That's right. Would you?" Fargo pursued.

"I don't know," the man said thoughtfully.

"You ought to think about it," Fargo said casually.

"Why?"

"Because if it happened, you'd have to move fast. It'd be best to have your mind made up," Fargo said.

"A lot of folks wouldn't go," Ned Calligan said. "They wouldn't leave everything they have to be burned to the ground."

"I'd take charred wood over new caskets," Fargo said.

"You've a hard way of putting things," Ned Calligan said, his brow creased in thought.

"Truth is hard," Fargo said.

"You expect Indian trouble? The Winnebago, the Saux, and the others around here have been quiet," the man said.

"They've new friends. The Sioux have come in from the plains," Fargo said and saw the dismay cloud Ned Calligan's face. "Think about it, friends," Fargo said as he rose to take his leave. When he was riding away, he knew the Calligans would talk to others, and they in turn would talk to more. Fargo had done what he wanted to do—he had planted the seed. He wanted them to know that the peace and quiet was just a mask. He wanted them to be ready for the worst, even if the worst never happened. He knew the dark prospects of being uninformed. They didn't need to know that much, not yet. It was enough that they become aware of the danger for now, and he had started that ball rolling.

It was late when he returned to Fort Cox. Every time the name of the fort passed through his mind, he grunted in derision. When he rode into the stockade he found Captain Duncan waiting for him. "We killed two Dakotas sneaking up on our outside sentries. Your instructions worked perfectly," the captain said.

"Good. That'll find its way back to Otaktay, too," Fargo said.

"I'm beginning to feel optimistic," Phil Duncan aid.

"You keep feeling that for the both of us," Fargo said and walked the Ovaro to the stables. Later, stretched out on the cot in the guest quarters, he allowed himself a feeling of a job well done, a good feeling to sleep on. In the morning, Lieutenant Jones and one of the sergeants took the patrol out. Fargo roamed the territory on his own, stopping to visit some more of the families he had passed the evening before. Once again, his eyes scanned every trail, tree, rock, and bush as he rode, probing every forest and high hill. Finally he circled his way back to Pebble Lake and found Joe Beaverhat washing clothes.

"I hear," the scout said.

"What do you hear?" Fargo asked.

"More attacks on patrols fail. More Dakota killed."

"How do you hear so much?" Fargo queried.

"Winnebago squaw friend. She listen, tell me," the scout said, a simple answer that revealed more than it overtly did.

"Tell her to keep listening," Fargo said.

"Otaktay very angry," Joe Beaverhat said and Fargo peered back. By now he had learned that the scout never simply made idle comments.

"What are you saying?" he asked.

"Otaktay have new respect for patrol soldiers. He not want to lose more warriors in unimportant raids," the scout said.

"That's exactly what I want," Fargo said.

"But he cannot lose respect. He must strike back, hit hard without losing many," Joe Beaverhat said.

Fargo stared for a moment as Joe Beaverhat's meaning stabbed into him, and he felt the chill sweep his body. "The settlers. He'll strike at the settlers." The scout nodded.

"Damn," Fargo spit out. "Thanks. I'll be back." He wheeled the pinto and sent the horse into a gallop, arriving at the fort before the sun went down. Fargo stormed into the captain's quarters. When he finished barking out the results of his meeting with Joe Beaverhat, the captain's face was drained of color.

"My God, we can't protect every one of them. There's no way. We'd spread ourselves too thin," the captain said.

"We'll have to pick one of the settlements and hope we have the right one," Fargo said.

"That'd be a shot in the dark, with more chance to guess wrong than right," Duncan said.

"No, we've a good chance to guess right. The Indian hunts by logic. He's learned not to chase a deer in another field when there's one in the woods close by. It's ingrained behavior. We pick the settlement closest to the Dakota camp," Fargo said.

Phil Duncan scowled in thought. "That'd be the Martins and the Greaveys. They settled farther north than anyone else. Martin, his wife, and brother, and two teenage sons run their farm. Greavey, his wife and two ten-year-olds live near them. They're real isolated."

"Perfect for the Dakota," Fargo said.

"I could surround both their places, put out a show of force that might discourage an attack," Duncan said.

"No," Fargo said. "I want the Dakota surprised and hurt. No show of force, but get your men together now."

"Now?"

"I figure the Dakota will attack by day, maybe as soon as tomorrow. That gives us tonight to move the Martins and Greaveys out and set up your men inside their cabins.

The captain's face lightened. "The Dakota will expect they'll be attacking two families. Instead, they'll get a barrage of carbine fire."

"Exactly," Fargo said. "Let's move." The captain, galvanized into action, strode outside and in no time, Fargo rode beside him at the head of a column of thirty-five troopers. They rode in silence through the darkness until they reached the two cabins where they surprised the astonished occupants. Ten of the troopers escorted the Martins and Greaveys back to the fort, leaving thirty-five troopers at the cabins. Duncan put ten in each cabin and had fifteen hide with their mounts in a thicket of black walnut some fifty yards behind the cabins. The moon was sliding its way toward the horizon when Fargo settled himself beside the captain inside the Martins' cabin. All the preparations were in place, the troopers inside the cabin lying silently on the floor. Fargo catnapped as the last hours of the night ticked away, and woke with the first slanting rays of the morning sun, gazing out across the quiet fields.

It was but a few minutes later that three soldiers clothed in overalls, workshirts, and straw hats took to the fields with shovels and rakes, and began to till the ground. It would be a perfectly normal, natural scene the Dakota were presented with when they arrived at the cabins, appearing suddenly out of the trees at the other side of the field. It was also only natural for the three figures to drop their tools and run in panic to the cabins, which they did in a convincing fashion. The Dakota force, some thirty strong, charged, their war whoops splitting the air. They raced forward with reckless confidence. Fargo noted two of the attackers light arrows coated with grease. He rose at the window of the cabin, the big Henry in hand as the captain shouted the command to fire.

A barrage of gunfire erupted from the windows and the door of the cabin was thrown open. The fusillade slammed into the charging Dakota, a vicious barrage that caused the attackers to rein up as though they had crashed into an invisible wall. Fargo's target, one of the braves with the fire arrow, flew from his pony as he glimpsed at least ten more of the attackers drop from their mounts. They were still trying to regroup, gripped by surprise, when the fifteen troopers raced from the trees behind the cabins. They laid down a concentrated channel of fire, and Fargo saw another half-dozen near-naked forms hit the ground.

The Dakota turned, fleeing in disarray, losing another five warriors as they did. In accordance with the captain's orders, the mounted troops didn't pursue the retreating braves further than the end of the tilled farmland. Captain Duncan's shout of triumph filled the air as Fargo stepped outside with him. "Perfect, absolutely perfect!" he exulted, and Fargo couldn't help the feeling of satisfaction that swept through him. The victory would hurt the Dakotas. It might be the act that would buy him the time he wanted. The Dakota chief was committed to wipe out the settlers and the fort. Fargo had no illusions that would change. But perhaps this would make Otaktay pull back, and rethink his plans. Fargo would be grateful for that much. Time was still the key to survival.

"Let's go back and return the Martins and Greaveys to their homes," the captain said. Fargo rode beside him as they went to the fort, where an escort took the two families back to their cabins. Fargo caught up on his sleepless night, and when he awoke, he had to fight joining Phil Duncan's optimism. "You're being too pessimistic," Duncan said. "You wanted to buy time. You've bought it. I'm sending a courier to General Davis with another request for more troops."

"Nothing to lose by that," Fargo said. "Give me

twenty men tomorrow. I want to teach them about fighting the Indian in open field combat. It'll come to that one of these times."

"They'll be ready for you," Duncan said and had the squad waiting for him when the next morning came. Fargo took them out into an open field, and instructed them in how to counter the Indian's quick strikes and wheeling-away tactics.

"Should we wheel with them, match our moves to theirs?" a sergeant queried.

"No. It's a good idea, but it won't work. Your army mounts can't turn as quickly as their ponies. General Davis developed a method that's effective. You let them wheel away and when they turn to swipe at you again, you pull up and fire. You'll catch them coming in every time," Fargo explained, then led the squad in a series of mock maneuvers that put his explanation into practice. When afternoon came, he led another squad through the same set of maneuvers until the day drew to a close. The captain sent his courier off to General Miles under cover of darkness and Fargo slept comfortably, allowing himself satisfaction if not optimism.

It was midmorning when Joe Beaverhat appeared at the fort the next day, and Fargo met him just outside the gate. "What have you heard?" he asked the scout.

"Not hear anything," Joe Beaverhat said.

Fargo's eyes narrowed at him. "Why'd you come?" he asked as apprehension swept over at him.

"Not hear anything, not see anything. No war parties, no scouting bands, not even lone Dakota hunter," the scout replied. Fargo peered at the man's impassive, broad-cheeked face as he turned the words over in his mind. Joe Beaverhat was delivering a message in his visual oblique way. Fargo felt the trepidation growing inside him. "What's it mean to you?" he asked.

"Wolf quiet when he prepares to attack," the scout said, the truth again delivered indirectly, wrapped in wisdom-filled metaphors. Fargo felt a terrible chill course through his veins.

"What if you read signs wrong?" Fargo asked.

"What if I read signs right?" the scout returned, and Fargo swore under his breath. Joe Beaverhat's answers were like a grim specter, his comment sealing the matter.

"I'll go see, maybe I'll get the answers we're looking for," Fargo said. It was the only way, he realized, and a way he had to take. Joe Beaverhat rode with him as far as Pebble Lake. Fargo rode on alone, his eyes watching the sun lower and he put the pinto into a canter. He halted at the cluster of aspens, tethered the Ovaro, and began to crawl his way through the tall, thick milk-thistles. The sun had reached the horizon when he came in sight of the Indian camp, and he crawled as close as he dared, letting his eyes again sweep the length of it. He spotted the Dakota chief in the center of the camp, surrounded by a dozen braves. He wore the same outfit, leggings and the bear claw necklace against his broad chest, his tall figure impressive, his physique and bearing befitting that of a true warrior chief. But Fargo had crawled close enough to have a better view of the cruel set to the man's mouth, the harsh lines that held his face in an icy mold. Otaktay held a long stick in one hand, and he was drawing in the soil with it. From his prone position in the weeds, Fargo could only see the chief drawing shorter marks, then more long lines in the soil, and he saw the braves gathered around him nodding, gesturing, asking questions.

Fargo's eyes shifted, halting at the rows of long boxes. They no longer held the rifles. The weapons had apparently been handed out, and Fargo moved his gaze on to where a row of braves were binding arrowheads to shafts with soaked, thinly cut threads of rawhide. The threads would dry out, holding the arrowheads firmly to the shafts. Fargo moved his focus further to the far end of the camp as dusk began to lower, concentrating on the rows of Indian ponies on their long tethers. A half-dozen braves had begun the task of painting various signs and symbols on the ponies, an important ritual before the sturdy ponies would carry their riders into battle.

They used the same dyes they used on their own bodies, made of colors pressed from red and purple berries, the yellow ochre of sand mixed with beaver oil and water, the dark browns and blacks fashioned from indelible walnut dye, birch bark, and fish oil. He brought his gaze back to the camp, scanning the length of it to the other side as the last of the day softly lit the sky. That's when he saw the dozen or so squaws seated on the ground, surrounded by stacks of dried grass. As he watched, they snapped the dry grass into even lengths, making compact bundles tied together by a length of hempen twine. Fargo cursed softly. Each bundle would become a burning fireball when tossed into the fort and onto the wooden stockade and roofs inside. They'd have hundreds, he saw, too many for the fort's defenders to stamp out. The dusk dropped away as darkness descended, and he saw cooking fires lighted.

He lay still, his thoughts on what he had seen. It had been more than enough to turn his stomach into a knot. Yet he wanted to see the marks Otaktay had drawn in the soil for the dozen braves who would make up his squad leaders. The Dakota chief returned to his teepee and the braves drifted off, but the markings in the soil remained. Fargo stretched out in the thick, tall stalks and prepared to wait. He lay still as a rock, listening to the sounds from the camp. He grew tense as a group of squaws wandered into the milk-thistle, but soon they went on their way, back to the camp. The night hours moved on and the faint light from the cooking fires was extinguished, all except one in the center of the camp that was left to remain a bed of burning embers to use come morning.

The camp finally grew still, and Fargo rose and started to crawl forward beyond the last row of the tall weeds, his eyes sweeping the camp for any sign of movement. The camp was covered with sleeping figures outside of the teepees, but he crept to the edge and waited, seeing no signs of movement, and then went on. Inching his way through the camp, he slid past figures half covered by blankets, finally arriving at the spot where Otaktay had drawn in the soil. Lifting himself onto his elbows, he let his eyes slowly move across the lines and markings that had been drawn. Though the tracings were stiff and crude, he saw they took on form and shape, becoming a pattern, almost like a map. Little squares had been outlined in different places and long lines were drawn to each cluster of squares. His eyes followed the lines as they moved to other squares, then still others, executing a series of curves that crossed each other.

It took him a few moments as he studied the long lines and the other marks, but it all suddenly fell together, forming a kind of crude blueprint, and Fargo felt an iciness sweep through his body. It was a blueprint for death—savage, merciless doom. The marks burned into Fargo's eye, becoming not lines and squares and meaningless squiggles but homes, settlers, farms and families. They also became the trails of racing warriors and the walls of a fort consumed in flames. He stared at the markings, saw how they pinpointed the settlements, how the lines clearly marked the paths that would be used by each attacking band of warriors. Otaktay intended to live up to the meaning of his name.

Tearing his eyes from the marks drawn in the soil, Fargo lowered himself again and began to crawl from the camp. Again, he forced himself to inch his way, aware that one mistake, one stone dislodged and sent rolling, would spell his demise. When he reached the tall milk-thistle, his body was soaked in perspiration and he lay still for a moment, drawing in deep drafts of air. He moved forward through the weeds again, reached the Ovaro, and climbed into the saddle. His ride back through the night was a ride through a similar and foreboding curtain. The markings drawn into the ground at the camp unsettled him as he realized they meant more than what they had said. They meant that everything he had done had turned on him, his past success now reversed, destined to become failure.

He forced himself to push away the despondent thoughts, to organize what he had seen and learned into bitter order. The marks in the soil demanded he start there. They were battle plans that had been drawn and left in place for others to study again, to familiarize themselves with. That meant it was not to be put into immediate action, and his thoughts went to the squaws and the fire bundles. From the small mountain of dry grass beside them, he guessed the squaws would have at least two days more work to complete their neat fire bundles. His thoughts shifted to the braves that had started painting the ponies.

They'd stop with the night, then start again when daylight came. They also would have at least two days' work before they finished painting every pony, perhaps three. Properly marking each pony was important. This attack was not to be an ordinary raid. This attack was to be the blow that signaled a new beginning for the tribes that had banded together. It would not be undertaken without the proper signs and symbols on every pony and rider, to bring proper protection and ensure victory. They'd not be finished with the task before three days, he guessed.

Lastly, an attack this important would demand a full spirit dance to the gods of war and victory. That, too, would be an imperative. The proper spirits had to be invoked, the shaman's rites employed, the long and enervating dances and rituals performed. He estimated that would take at least one more night with perhaps another day to recuperate. Fargo added the pieces together and came up with four, maybe five, days before the Dakota chief would send his warriors on that final, all-out attack.

The night drew on and when he finally reached the fort, he had made his conclusions, formed his plans, and hated himself for it.

8

Phil Duncan was still up when Fargo pounded on the door of his quarters. He answered the door, and instantly saw the hard line of his visitor's jaw. "Trouble," he said.

"More than trouble," Fargo said. "Curtain time. They're getting ready to attack." The captain sat back heavily into his chair and Fargo paced the little room in front of him. "Everything I've done, all the successes, the training, it's all backfired. You could say we're paying the price for being successful."

"How do you mean?" Duncan inquired.

"It didn't make Otaktay back off. It didn't make him slow down. None of it bought us any time at all. Instead, he decided his best course was an all-out attack, a full-scale war, and not more raids to pick you apart and weaken you. I didn't figure on that reaction from him, damn his soul," Fargo said.

"He'll attack the fort, of course, with everything he has," Duncan said.

"He's going to wipe out the settlers, first. He's got

his plans all ready. They won't have a chance," Fargo said.

"When?" the captain asked.

"I figure in four, maybe five days."

Phil Duncan groaned. "We can't protect them. We can't spread our troopers over that wide an area. Maybe we could pick out a dozen or so, put a sizeable force around them."

"You going to choose who gets the call and who will be left to die?" Fargo asked.

The captain put his hands to his face. "No, I couldn't. I know them all. I couldn't choose."

"You can bring every family out there into the fort," Fargo said.

The captain brought his hands down, and stared back, thinking. "We could. We've room enough," he finally said.

"They'll be massacred if they stay in their homes," Fargo warned.

The captain's lips thinned. "You know, they'll likely meet the same end here," he said with grim honesty.

Fargo nodded. "But with less brutality, less torture. They'll accept that. It's a time for small favors." The captain let out a deep sigh of bitter agreement. "You'll bring them into the fort by night, every last one of them."

"After that we dig in and wait and try to fight them off, though we both know there's little chance we can do that," the captain said, resignation replacing the bitterness in his voice.

"I'll be riding out come dawn," Fargo said.

"Don't blame you. You've done all you could. There's no reason for you to stay here and die. Miles Davis didn't send you to be a martyr," the Captain said.

"Didn't say I was finished. If you had a hundred more bodies to throw against the Dakota, you'd have a chance. I'm going to try and get them for you while there's still time," Fargo said as the captain's eyes widened.

"How? Where?" he asked hopefully.

"Best you don't ask yet. I'll be reaching out to unexpected places," Fargo said tightly, and Phil Duncan saw that he'd get nothing more from the big man. He didn't try, and was glad to embrace any prospect of help.

"See you in time, I hope. Start bringing in some of the families tonight. Tell them to come with their wagons, their guns, and their clothes, nothing else," Fargo said. "You won't have room for personal possessions."

The captain nodded and Fargo strode from the office, went to the guest quarters, and lay down on the cot. He slept deeply until the first light of the new day woke him. Rising, he dressed, went outside, and led the Ovaro to the gate. He saw four farm wagons lined up, a half-dozen youngsters up and out before their elders and he paused, taking in the innocent, smooth-cheeked faces, filled with eager curiosity at their new surroundings. There were so many others still outside, unaware of how little of their lives were hanging unfinished.

Fargo turned away from their sweet, open faces,

swung almost angrily onto the Ovaro, and rode from the fort. He headed the horse south across open land as the sun rose higher, riding with a terrible heaviness inside him. The feeling would stay, he knew, no matter what the final outcome. But desperate moments made for desperate measures, he told himself, and realized that truth was no guarantee of absolution. Keeping a steady pace, Fargo reached the open land east of the Mud River, following it west until he neared the Thief River. He scanned the horizon as he rode, his lips pulled back in distaste. He knew he went forward depending on certain assumptions—one, that Amity would have made initial mistakes in breaking trail; and two, that she had corrected those errors and swung the herd north. He didn't like going on assumptions, but he had nothing else, and his calculations told him that she would have been able to cross the Thief by now.

As he rode, Fargo climbed every rise that could provide a better view of the land as it stretched out far beyond. But he did not spot any herd slowly moving over the flat terrain, and as day drew to a close he halted beside a pond. He lay down with the darkness, let himself take in a few hours of solid rest, and when he woke the moon was well across the midnight sky. He took to the saddle again under a three-quarter moon that bathed the plains with enough light to discern anything fairly close, but nothing distant. Yet he rode, trusting not the power of moonlight or the strength of his eyes, but the night wind that blew gently but steadily across the land.

He steered the horse in a pattern from left to right and back again so he could cover all the land before him, each time progressing another few hundred yards forward. It was slow going and it put a strain on his patience, but he doggedly stayed with it. His lips drawn back, Fargo had to wonder if he had guessed right. Amity could have turned further west, he knew, or followed a wrong trail. He was gambling he was right, but not just for himself. His was a gamble for the lives of the young, innocent towheaded children and their parents who had thought themselves in a safe and protected land. And, he gambled for the lives of the young soldiers put in the wrong place for the wrong reasons by men who now abandoned them. High stakes, he grunted bitterly, too high for gambling. Yet a gamble was all he had left.

He had to trust instinct and experience and Amity's determination and ability to correct her mistakes. He guessed he had ridden another three hours into the night when he slowed the Ovaro, his nostrils suddenly quivering. Drawing in a deep breath, Fargo caught the scent, a distinct murky, dark, odor, a smell all of itself made of wool and hide and sweat, that unique, special odor of cattle in large numbers. He felt excitement pull at him. The scent drifted to him from his left and he turned the horse toward it, keeping the mount at a walk. The scene grew stronger, unmistakable, unlike any other. Following his nose, he continued to keep the pinto at a walk and slowly, the dark shape came into sight, spread out in a still circle. It took on features, and Fargo finally discerned cattle at rest for the night. Straining into the dark, he saw four range hands positioned around the edges of the herd, on nighthawk duty, as cowboys called it. He edged the Ovaro toward the nearest hand sitting half asleep atop his horse when a frown pressed into his brow.

Fargo felt his nostrils flare as the wind sent another odor drifting to him, the dark, dank, pungent odor he had memorized earlier. It plainly came from the horse and rider in front of him, and Fargo slid silently from the saddle. Moving in a crouch, he stepped nearer to the horse and rider, close enough to get a good look at the man in the saddle. He was not one of the young men Amity had riding herd for her. This man was older, in his thirties, Fargo guessed, a lined face with half-closed eyes set in deep sockets. Fargo drew in the pungent odor again and then quietly drew away.

Another night guard sat atop his horse at the far end of the herd, and Fargo crept toward him on steps silent as a cougar on the prowl. As he neared the guard in the dark, the pungent odor grew stronger again and circling, he peered closely at the man. He was not one of Amity's hands, either, a pudgy figure at least forty years old with a piggish face. Fargo paused, his eyes searching the other end of the herd, seeing a third nighthawk in place. He needed no more to recognize real trouble. These weren't Amity's men and he let his eyes slowly move along the edge of the herd, finally spotting a knot of figures asleep on the ground. Straining his eyes, he counted eight sleeping forms as apprehension curled through him. He searched along a line of scrubby bushes that looked a little like misplaced mountain brush. He had almost reached the last of the shrubs when he found more shapes in a line in front of the bushes, lying one next to the other. He dropped to his hands and knees and crawled forward, passing the horseman and creeping on until he neared the line of figures.

A shock of red hair, a pale echo of its usual self under the moonlight yet vibrant enough to leap out at him, caught his eye. Creeping closer, he reached Amity. She lay on her back, her eyes closed, fatigue in her face, and Fargo saw that her wrists and ankles were bound. She was tied to the young man beside her by a rope that ran from her neck to his. Fargo glanced down the line of figures, seeing neck ropes tying each of them together. He put one hand over Amity's mouth. She awoke instantly, her eyes growing wide as she focused on him. He kept his hand over her mouth until she nodded in understanding, then he drew his hand away.

Taking the thin, double-bladed toothpick knife from its calf holster, he severed the wrist and ankle ropes, then the length of rope that bound her to the figure beside her. She sat up, clung to him instantly, arms tight around his neck in a wordless yet fervent embrace. When he pulled back, he motioned to the young man beside her and she leaned over, waking him, touching one finger to her lips. He stared back incredulously as Fargo used the knife to cut him free. "Wake the others," he whispered and the man woke the figure next to him. The man sat up and woke the man beside him as Fargo went from one to another severing their bonds. Finally they were all cut free and Fargo leaned forward, keeping his voice a barely audible whisper. He motioned to where the knot of figures slept a dozen yards away. "Take care of them. Quick and quiet. No shouting," he whispered.

The men nodded and began to crawl to the knot of sleeping figures. They'd seize a gun and use the butt or they'd use their hands, striking with silent mercilessness. Fargo crouched, his eyes on the guard by the cattle. As he expected, the man heard or sensed something, and prodded his horse toward the front of the herd. He never saw Fargo's figure slicing through the darkness at him as he passed. The blow from the Colt, smashing into his temple, sent him toppling from his horse. The man landed hard, and Fargo caught the sound of vertebrae snapping. He turned away and Amity was suddenly in his arms, clinging to him as he peered through the dark to where her young hands were wreaking their fury on those who had taken them captive. They included the other guard on horseback, who had come riding back at the sound. When they straggled back to where he waited with Amity, he saw the mixture of shame and relief on their faces.

"What happened?" Fargo asked Amity.

"They rode up friendly, but then they pulled guns and took us," Amity said. "It was all so sudden."

"They were part of the same crowd who attacked you before. The odor was on their horses, too," Fargo said.

"I know. I smelled it, but it was too late," Amity said.

"Why didn't they just kill you? Why were they dragging all of you along with them?" Fargo queried.

"They wanted no one left around. They were waiting to find a lake to throw us in after they finished. They promised me a good time, first," Amity said with a bitter snort.

"I don't think it's Baxter Carter," Fargo said. "I can't be sure, but I've my doubts."

She shrugged. "Others knew about my cattle," Amity said. He turned to the young hands.

"Finish the night out. We'll go on in the morning," he said and they walked away, leaving Amity clinging to his arm. She pulled him down to a patch of gama grass with her.

"Why are you here? I'm afraid to ask, really," she said.

"To break trail for you. I told you I would soon as I got the chance," he said. Her arms flew around him and he felt the warmth of her lips on his as little half sobs shook from her.

"Yes, you did, but I'd stopped believing," Amity said, pulling back and searching his face. "You've a way of always coming back when I need you most."

"Part of it's plain luck," Fargo said.

"A wonderful kind of luck," Amity answered and her mouth found his, barely controlling her ardent fervor. He saw her lust thrashing inside herself when she pulled back, throwing a quick glance at where the cowhands stretched out on the ground. "Too close," he heard her mutter, her tone a grumble.

"For what?" he asked.

"For whatever," she said and she turned her back to him, pulled his arms around her waist, and fitted herself against him. "Good night," she whispered and was asleep against him in moments. Exhaustion was an effective impediment to everything, he knew and he lay still with her, feeling his own lips pull back in a grimace of distaste. He'd hold off telling her the things he didn't dare. But it was going to get harder for her. She'd not be alone in that, he grunted unhappily and finally fell asleep himself.

Morning came with a searing sun and Fargo rose first, and was already instructing the hands when Amity came up. "I'll be ahead scouting trails. For now, you just keep the herd moving and take it slow," he said.

"I'd like to ride along," Amity put in and he nodded his consent, turning back to the hands. "You just keep moving due east," he said.

"East?" Amity frowned. "No, we've got to keep going north."

"Thought I was going to break trail for you," Fargo said mildly.

She colored for a second. "Sorry," she said. "East it is."

"I'll explain later," Fargo said. "Let's ride." He started the Ovaro east and put the horse into a trot, and she caught up to him after a few moments. He was aware she watched him closely as he scanned the distant land, following him closely as he crested a rise to get a better view.

"You're looking for something in particular," Amity noted, and he smiled at her sharpness.

"First thing's a lake," Fargo said. "Your cattle are dried out." She frowned at him, concern instantly leaping across her face. "You can hear it in the way they bellow and see it in the way they swallow," he said.

"I haven't stopped enough. I've been pushing hard to make time. I guess I lost sight of basics," Amity said.

"You can't drive cattle like that on a long haul. They need watering," Fargo said.

"I could use some myself," Amity said, and stayed close as he rode from the rise to cross low land again. The withering sun beat down on them. "You were going to explain why you're heading the herd east," she reminded him.

He expected the question, yet he chose his words carefully. He wanted to be logical, sincere, and convincing. "There's big trouble you never expected," he said. "An Indian uprising, led by the Yankton Dakota. I've been riding the land. They're all over, especially to the north. I'm going to take you around the worst of them if I can."

"I always heard Indians aren't into cattle rustling," Amity said.

"Not the way white men rustle. But they're into wool and hides for clothing, and meat to dry for the winter. Your herd would be a banquet for them in every one of those ways," Fargo said.

"Yes, I suppose so," Amity said gravely. She leaned over, reaching out to touch his cheek with one hand. "I came to hire you because they said you were the best. I didn't know how much they were right." She drew her touch away and he put the Ovaro into a canter. They'd gone over another hour when he caught the sparkle of blue through a forest of basswood. Fargo exploded along the side of the forest at once, trying to see if there was a way around the trees that could accommodate the large herd. He found one, where the forest separated into two sections, the space large enough for the herd to pass through. He rode forward to the edge of the crystal-clear, L-shaped lake and reined to a halt. "We've plenty of time before the herd gets anywhere near here," she said.

"Time for what?" he asked.

"For everything," Amity said, swinging from the saddle and walking to the edge of the water on a carpet of dark green nut moss that grew right up to the softly lapping waves. She turned to face him as he dismounted, and he saw her begin to unbutton her shirt. The garment fell open in moments, revealing the long, curved sides of her breasts. With a wriggle of her shoulders, she shed the blouse completely, facing him with eyes darkened in a kind of smoldering pride. She stood very straight and he let his eyes move slowly over the tall beauty of her. She had skin common to flaming redheads, milky white and smooth even to the eye, with a trace of freckles on her shoulders. Nicely rounded shoulders, he noted, ribs long but narrow, her full breasts curving smoothly and gracefully.

Her small, reddish nipples were already thrusting forward firmly. Centered on pale pink, small areolas,

Fargo noticed that they gave her breasts a little-girl look to them. Still standing very tall and quiet, she pushed her skirt and half-slip down with one, quick movement to stand beautifully naked before him. Fargo started appreciating her beauty once again. Her narrow waist moved downward into wide, womanly hips that in turn curved down to long, lovely legs, her milky white thighs both full yet slender. A very full and unruly, rose-hued nap echoed the carrot red head of hair as a painter echoes color from one place to another on a canvas.

She turned, walking very straight, her breasts swaying together, and reached into her saddlebag and came out with a bar of beef fat soap. She stepped into the lake and lowered herself into the water. Fargo watched her dive under the surface her rear end rising up in a beautiful, tight mound. Then she vanished into the water. She surfaced, and he began to pull off his clothes as Amity began to use the soap on herself. She had finished lathering when he strode into the lake. She tossed him the soap and disappeared under the surface again, swimming out further, then back, her arms graceful arcs with each stroke. He had thrown the soap onto the shore when she rose up in the water in front of him, little droplets provocatively hanging from each reddish nipple. She came to him, her arms encircling his neck, the silk-smooth touch of her breasts rubbing against his chest.

He bent down, scooped her from the water, and carried her to the soft carpet of moss, his mouth finding hers, then sliding down to one milky white breast. He drew the mound into his mouth, gently caressed the tip with his tongue, circling the tiny, thin, threadlike little hairs the circled the areola. "Oh, oh my God, oh," Amity gasped out, her hands digging into his back. He kissed, caressed, and pulled gently with his mouth, enjoying the smooth feel of her, and heard her gasps building to small cries. She pressed her back against the moss and pushed upward, thrusting her breast deeper into his mouth. As his lips held her firm, thrusting little nipple, his hand slid downward, across her concave, long stomach, creeping over her flat abdomen, edging the shallow rise of her pubic mound.

"Oh, oh, Jeez, oh my God," Amity half screamed, her legs stretching out stiffly, then arching up, turning together from one side to the other. Reaching down further, he pressed his palm against the soft mound under her rosy bush, enjoying again how the unruly, soft fibrous hairs sprang up around his fingers. Amity's torso continued to twist and her cries grew louder. He slid his palm further downward, sliding from her downy bush and reaching the silky slit between her legs, halting, resting as Amity's voice rose to a scream. "Ah . . . aaaaaaah, aaaaiiiieee," she cried out and he felt the surprising softness of her. He inched further to where he could touch her dark, warm moistness and Amity's fists struck against his ribs and shoulders, and pounded on the mossy carpet.

A kind of helpless frenzy came over her and as he touched deeper, striking the portal of all sweet ecstasy, her screams rose again. She pulled at him, her hands alternately clutching and scratching and her hips writhed, rose, and lifted, her senses pleading. Her milky white thighs quickly reddened at the force with which she clamped them around his hand and rubbed up and down along his hips. Low, strangled words tore from her: "Now, now, now . . . take me, God, take me, take me damn you!" The low sounds were transformed into a scream as his throbbing warmth rose and came against her, pressing into her rosebush nap. Her thighs fell open, her hips lifted and he slid forward, the glorious path made welcome with the nectar of the body, their senses afire in confirmation of desire. He slid deeper and Amity seemed to explode, becoming a frenzy of thrusting, twisting, tossing, arms and legs clamping, seizing, her longish breasts falling from one side to the other, her carrot red hair flying in all directions.

It was as though he were suddenly with a creature gone wild, past all control, her body an erupting thing of its own, every fiber of her quivering, trembling, her cries of ecstasy gone beserk. Carried along by her wild fervor, he plunged and thrusted to match her wild abandon when he felt her suddenly stiffen, then slam herself against him, her teeth digging into his shoulder. As her scream spiraled across the lake, he was ready to explode with her. "Yes, yes, yes! Fargo, Fargo, oh, my God, now, now now!" Amity screamed, the sound a strange combination of a wild laugh and a cry of despair. Amity was a Medusa, Circe, Lilith, a wild creature able to absorb only a part of the sensual ecstasy that seized control of her. She screamed again, then again, and once more and then her cry broke in midair, becoming a shuddered lament that ended against his chest.

She lay there, a part of her holding him in a soft vise until finally he felt her thighs grow limp and fall away from his body. She sank down into herself, not unlike a balloon with the air sucked from it, every part of her spent, depleted. He stayed with her, still savoring the tactile pleasure of skin against skin until she stirred, then pulled back, her dark blue eyes wide with a kind of wonder too powerful to understand. "Too much, too wonderful," Amity murmured. She saw his smile as he studied her. "What is it?" she asked.

"Red hair," he said. "Powerful stuff."

Her breasts lifted as she shrugged, her little smile holding its own secrets inside itself. "Nothing halfway, hating or loving, fighting or fucking," she said. He smiled in wry agreement. She certainly lived up to her words. She pulled his head to her, rested his lips on one tiny nipple. "It's been more than I ever expected. When it's over I won't have words for it," she said.

She didn't see the tightness come into his face. "You'll find them," he said and somehow managed to keep the grimness from his voice. Tomorrow swam into his thoughts. He hadn't created the pain that waited. He hadn't set the terrible wheels in motion. Only his part of it. That was burden enough.

9

Amity was dressed and running a brush through her hair as Fargo rode out to meet the herd. He took them through the break in the basswood forest and to the lake, and had the hands spread the cattle around its entire perimeter. It avoided injuries that could come with too many powerful bodies fighting for space and water. Spread out, the cattle were content to drink leisurely and stay in place. He circled the shoreline to where Amity waited with the young hands. "I don't like what I've been seeing as we rode," Fargo said to Amity but included the others. "I'm going to bring the herd close to Fort Cox for safety."

"Whatever you think best," Amity agreed quickly. Fargo nodded and refused to let the turmoil inside himself reach him. He gave the cattle another hour to let the water they had consumed settle in their stomachs. The afternoon had already began to draw to a close when he had the hands round up the cattle, and he led the way east again, Amity riding at his side. There was no safe way to hurry the herd, nor did he want to do so. He had decided that he'd thrown the dice. Things would go the way he had calculated, the timetable falling into place, or it was all for nothing. The final gamble hung over his head like a dark thunder cloud.

Later, when night descended, Amity settled against him. He had noticed how she scanned the terrain as they rode, how her aquiline beauty remained calm and relaxed. Trust and confidence in him had wiped away all her fears and apprehensions. The hour beside the lake had only been a seal on her feelings. He was responsible for how she felt. But what should have been a rewarding feeling for him was only a knot of bitterness. He cursed a world that gave choices that were really no choices at all, that put right and wrong, winning and losing, on the same side of the coin.

When morning came, he moved the herd on and counted off the hours. Leaving Amity with the herd, he went out on a half-dozen sorties to study the land on his own, scanning the distance and examining the marks where he rode. He knew that when the Indians struck, when they won their bloody victory, they'd send roving bands far and wide scouring the countryside. They would proclaim the new day that had dawned as their day of bloody glory. But the tracks of unshod pony prints that he saw told him that hadn't happened. He found nothing to turn hope into ashes. His timetable was still in place and he returned to the herd and Amity.

"I was getting worried about you," she said with a glance at the oncoming dusk.

"Not yet," he said and she leaned over to brush his

cheek with her lips. "We won't be stopping for the night," he told her.

"I'll tell the hands," she said and rode away. Fargo's eyes cut to the horizon where the sun was beginning to lower. Another handful of hours would bring the final moment, the last turn of the wheel of chance. He would have to live with the results. Or die by them. He and everyone else. He rode on feeling a bond with all those before him whom fate had thrust into making decisions they never sought to make. There was no glory in the feeling, he realized now, only righteousness and guilt, a mixture made in hell, never to be reconciled.

"You're very quiet," Amity noticed as she rode beside him.

"I'm listening," Fargo said curtly and she fell silent. The moon had marked the midnight sky, he saw, and reined up. The fort was only a half hour away. "I'll be going on alone. Stay with the herd till I get back," he said. She leaned from the saddle, her lips warm and full of tenderness. They stayed clinging to each other for a moment longer, then he rode off, putting the pinto into a fast canter. He slowed when he reached the fort and immediately noticed there were no tents outside the walls. He walked the horse forward across the open land, and saw the gate open as he neared it. He rode in to see the compound crowded with small pup tents, figures sleeping on the ground, small circles of families gathered in corners or in the open, wherever space permitted. An extra complement of sentries lined the walls, he saw, and an open path was cleared for quick troop movements.

Lieutenant Jones came forward as he dismounted. "The captain up?" Fargo asked.

"Definitely. None of us get much sleep these nights," Jones said and Fargo saw the words reflected in the drawn tired lines of his face. "It's been quiet," the lieutenant said. "But the waiting has everybody chewing nails."

"The waiting's over," Fargo said, seeing Phil Duncan peer at him.

"You're back alone," the captain said.

"No, the others are waiting," Fargo said.

"You brought reinforcements?" Duncan said, his eyes widening with instant hope.

"In a way," Fargo said and began to throw words out, spelling out what he had done and the plans he had laid out in his desperate gamble. He watched both men's eyes darken in a combination of astonishment and disbelief. When he finished, Phil Duncan stumbled about finding words.

"It's sure as hell not what I expected," he muttered.

"I promised you a hundred more bodies to throw at the Dakota. I didn't say what kind," Fargo answered.

"You really think this will work?" Duncan frowned.

"It's the only thing that can. You can't run, not with all those people outside, and you can't fight them off here. There are too many and this place isn't strong enough. This is the only chance. You'll have the advantage of surprise, too," Fargo said.

Phil Duncan turned his palms upward. "I've nothing better," he conceded. "Spell out the details, what you want us to do and how."

Fargo took a sheet of paper on the desk, and using the captain's pencil drew a diagram, beginning with the Dakota camp, then the herd and the position for each of the squads. "Leave the settlers here with a skeleton force. Take everybody else. There'll be no need to hold back. This is for everything. We win or lose here," he said.

Duncan nodded grimly. "The young woman with the herd, how'd you get her to go along with this?" he questioned.

"I didn't," Fargo said and left it at that.

"I'll get the men briefed and mounted. I'd guess we'll be meeting within the half hour," the captain said and Lieutenant Jones nodded agreement.

"Good enough," Fargo said and hurried out to the pinto. He rode back at a fast canter and Amity came forward to meet him when he reached the herd. He put just the right amount of concern in his face as he realized how quickly it became easy to lie. You just had to convince yourself you had a good enough reason. "It's not good. There are Dakota bands roving all over. They're on the warpath. You'll never get through on your own," he told her. "I've arranged a cavalry escort."

Surprise flooded her face. "How'd you do that?"

"Captain Duncan owes me a favor and I convinced him it'd be smart to stop the tribes from getting clothes and food for the winter," Fargo said.

Amity leaned against him. "You know, I'll never forget you for this," she murmured.

"I know," he said and was glad she didn't catch the bitterness in his voice. He motioned, calling the hands over to where he stood with Amity. "There'll be troops coming up. They'll take over driving the cattle. They'll ride mostly at the rear of the herd. That way they can move quickly in any direction if there's an attack. I want you to pull up behind them. You'll be out of the way there," he said, casting a glance at Amity. "That goes for you, too."

She nodded, glad to accept his instructions. "And you?" she asked.

"I'll be riding with the captain," he said. "Let's move."

He positioned himself at the front of the herd as they pressed on. Half an hour later, Fargo spotted the long columns of the troopers approaching them. "So many?" Amity frowned. "That looks like a full company."

"It is," Fargo said. "There are a lot of braves out there." He turned, separating from the herd along with Amity, the hands falling back to join the cattle as they moved slowly on their way. He watched the troopers take up their positions, one line on each side of the herd, a handful in front with the main body of riders swinging in behind the rear. Fargo rode beside Amity as the troopers herded the cattle forward, taking the slight curve northeast. As they moved on, Fargo's eyes lifted to the moon, and he watched it make its way down the starless sky, counting off the minutes as he rode. Timing was still the all-important, key factor. If they arrived too early, they'd be attacking while it was still dark, and would be unable to see their targets, the element of surprise made largely useless. Too late and the Dakota would be awake, and would be able to see them coming, the surprise once again would be useless. They had to reach the camp just as dawn bathed it in the first light of the new day.

Fargo felt his throat grow dry as he rode. They had passed Pebble Lake when he spotted a lone figure approaching from the left. He knew the captain would recognize the man's beaver hat even in the moonlight, and Fargo stayed beside Amity as the scout paused beside Duncan, letting the herd pass before coming alongside. Fargo's stomach knotted as the scout glanced at Amity. "Amity Baker. This is her herd," Fargo said, glancing at Amity. "This is Joe Beaverhat. He scouts for the army," he explained.

Amity tossed him a warm smile. "Fargo has been wonderful, arranging all this for me," she said.

Fargo kept his face expressionless under Joe Beaverhat's long, steady glance. "Fargo is man of many surprises," the scout said and Fargo let himself draw a deep relieved breath.

"I'll ride up forward with Joe," Fargo said, leaving Amity behind.

"Not see cattle like these before," the scout said as they passed the herd.

"Special old breed. Rare," Fargo said.

"Not see them again, I think," Joe Beaverhat said. Fargo needed no further explanation from the scout as

138

to his meaning. When they came abreast of Duncan, the captain nodded at Joe.

"You tell him what you're planning?" Duncan asked.

"Didn't need to," Fargo replied and Joe Beaverhat almost smiled.

"Welcome aboard. Every gun helps," Duncan said. "Where do you figure to be when it goes down?"

"Sharpshooting from the side," the scout said.

"Your choice," the captain said and with a nod to the scout, Fargo returned to Amity just as the moon began to dip behind the horizon.

"I'll be riding with the captain for a while. You stay back here where you'll be safe," he told her, then hurried away before she could do anything more than nod. Joe Beaverhat had slipped into the night when Fargo returned to the captain. The Trailsman peered forward as he rode, searching the darkness, and suddenly found the dark, tall forest of aspens. "The camp is coming up, directly in front of us," Fargo said, his eyes shifting to the first pink-gray streaks of the new day. The captain turned to Lieutenant Jones.

"Get to the rear. The sergeant at the left side has his orders. Fire when the camp comes into sight, then keep the herd going forward together. Don't let them spread out," Duncan ordered. The lieutenant nodded and rode away as Fargo watched dawn swiftly roll across the land. It was but a few minutes more that the land lay bathed in light, the still-sleeping Indian camp revealed by the rising crimson orange sun. Fargo's eyes scanned the silent length of it. His body tensed, waiting and ready, when a shot split the air, followed instantly by another shot, then another until the air rang with the clamor of gunfire. The sudden explosion of shots did exactly what they were meant to do. Fargo saw the mountain of white-gray fur erupt as the herd reared up, bellowing as they charged.

The earth shook, the atmosphere quivered, and the pounding hooves thundered forward, kept together by the lines of troopers on both sides of the herd. Fargo had his Colt in hand as near-naked figures began to burst from the teepees, running from every fire circle, springing up from every blanket. They grabbed rifles and bows but the mass of thundering cattle was already upon them, hurtling into the camp as more shots kept them in their headlong panic. He watched lines of braves disappear under the trampling hooves, teepees flattened and torn apart. But the Indians tried to gather themselves, seeing there'd be no turning the charging beasts aside. They fired into the herd in an effort to bring them down and stop their brutal stampede. Their fire took its toll, and Fargo saw the gray-white South Highland fur splattered with scarlet as the cattle fell.

In what seemed seconds, the ground was littered with blood-streaked cattle amid the shambles of what had been a camp. Many of the Indians tried to run for their ponies but were slaughtered by the troopers that raced down on them in full attack. Fargo brought down three fleeing Dakotas as they tried to run off to one side of their decimated camp. The troopers raced their horses back and forth, laying down a withering fire as the remains of the herd still charged among them, still overtaking fleeing braves and trampling them into the ground. Fargo saw a knot of braves shooting at the cattle in fury and frustration as Fargo moved the Ovaro forward. Riding around the mounds of fallen cattle, he also saw the corpses of crushed and broken naked bodies.

It was going well, better than he'd dared to hope. The troopers were running down Dakota warriors, still disarrayed by surprise and chaos. He caught sight of some escaping, fleeing on ponies they had managed to reach, with bands of troopers pursuing after them. His eye caught the movement to the right, beyond the camp, where a forest of black walnut rose. He sent the Ovaro around two bodies of slain steers, glancing back at the pockets of fighting that still raged on, his eyes returning to the figures disappearing into the black walnut. The rider leading the others into the forest flashed in front of him between two trees. Fargo saw his tall stature, his black hair flowing, sitting on his horse imperiously even as he fled.

Alarm spearing into him, Fargo sent the Ovaro into a gallop, ducking a volley of arrows that flew at him from the side as he rode by. Crossing the distance at an angle, Fargo drew closer to the fleeing Indians and caught the bouncing movement of the bear-claw necklace. They couldn't let the Dakota chief escape, Fargo knew, keeping the Ovaro at a full gallop. Otaktay had to be stopped here and now. If the Dakota chief survived, he would be a symbol, a rallying point for the Indian's pride. More than that, he would organize again, plot further attacks, and go back to gather new warriors. If he were left to survive, sooner or later he would return for his revenge. Their victory would be a temporary thing, a mere hiatus. If he lived, he would bring death again.

Fargo saw the Dakota chief fling a glance at him as he reached the edge of the trees. It was a quick but piercing look that said volumes in its brief flash. In it, the bloodthirsty Dakota chief said that he knew his pursuer was a special foe, and he understood what his pursuit meant. Otaktay knew in ways beyond logic or reasoned explanation. He knew as the hare knows when the hawk approaches. So when Fargo reached the forest, plunging into its full greenery, he found only silence, heavy foliage, and thick underbrush. He brought the pinto to a halt at once, his ears straining for the slightest sound. He was the Trailsman, and he knew what most men seldom learned. He knew that silence was not really silence at all, but only another form of sound, able to be understood and interpreted.

Sliding from the saddle, he crouched in a thick cluster of underbrush, staying motionless and still. The Indians had left their ponies, one assigned to keep the mounts quiet. That left Otaktay and three of his braves preparing to strike. Fargo remained stationary, waiting, and the sound came perhaps a few minutes later, the faint, subtle crackle of a blade of dry grass being pressed underfoot. He spun just as a figure appeared through the tall brush, half crouched, searching, a long-bladed hunting knife in one hand.

The Indian saw him just as he drew the Colt,

launching himself forward with a cry of triumph, the knife upraised to strike. Fargo dived but the Dakota twisted his body in the middle of the leap, and the shot missed. The leaping figure bowled into him and Fargo went down onto his back, and felt the knife tear through his shirt at the shoulder. He rolled, throwing the brave aside as he did, bringing the Colt up again as the man flung himself at him. This time the shot hit its target, and the brave shuddered as he pitched forward, then lay still on the ground, facedown. Fargo spun as he caught another sound behind him, that of leaves being brushed aside.

The second brave held a coarse-toothed bone skinning knife, and Fargo knew well what damage the weapon could do. He fired as the man rushed at him, two shots that caught his attacker full in the chest. The brave pitched forward as his chest exploded, falling almost in the same manner and position as the previous one, both now lying with outstretched arms touching each other, their faces pressed lifelessly into the ground. The third one came at Fargo from the side, rushing out of another clump of tall brush. Fargo's shot only grazed the Dakota's ribs, who also brandished a shining hunting knife. He slashed out with the weapon and Fargo ducked away, doing the same as the brave rushed again at him. The Indian whirled to slash at him again, but Fargo fired from one knee and the brave went down, both hands clutching his abdomen.

Fargo rose as a faint whistling sound caught his ear, and tried to duck away but the tomahawk caught him alongside the elbow. The Colt fell from his hand as he felt the numbness course through his arm. He saw the tall figure of Otaktay coming at him, and parried the blow that struck out at him. The Dakota chief came in recklessly, reaching out to close both hands around his foe's throat. Dropping down, Fargo avoided the hands that tired to wring his neck but Otaktay's body slammed into him with tremendous force. As he went down, Fargo felt the Indian's hands starting to curl around his neck. His right arm still numb from where the tomahawk had struck him, Fargo brought his left arm up, using the side of his fist with all the strength he could command. He smashed the blow into the bear-claw necklace, driving a half dozen of the sharp claws deep into the man's chest. Otaktay let out a roar of pain as he fell to one knee, grabbing at the claws imbedded into his chest.

With another roar of pain and fury, he ripped the claws free, starting to turn as his chest ran with blood. But Fargo had already scooped the Colt up, and firing with his left hand, he emptied the gun at the tall figure. The blood dripping from the bear claw wounds mingled with that from the wide gunshot wounds as the Dakota chief dropped to his knees, then fell forward onto his face. Fargo stared down at him.

"Otaktay," Fargo muttered. "One who kills many. But not anymore." Fargo listened for a moment to the sounds of a horse racing away through the forest, and knew it was the fourth brave who'd fled with Otaktay. Fargo pushed to his feet and climbed onto the Ovaro. He rode into the open, surveying the scene of fury and carnage. The gunfire had ended, and he took in the troopers presently holding small clusters of Dakota braves prisoner. Most of the Indians were now silent forms littering the ground. Fargo glimpsed the Winnebago and Kickapoo moccasin designs among those of the Dakotas. He rode across the remains of what had been their camp, making his way around the bodies of cattle piled high onto each other. Almost three-quarters of the herd, he guessed, were dead. The rest would be still running off somewhere.

He saw her red hair, first, then her tall figure wandering aimlessly among the mounds of slain cattle. He stopped beside her and saw the tearstains on her milky white cheeks as she looked up at him, her eyes wide and full of pain.

"What happened? What went wrong?" she asked.

"One of the troopers thought he saw an attack coming. He panicked and started shooting. It set everything off," Fargo said. Another lie wouldn't make any difference, he told himself, not now. Truth wouldn't help, and it wouldn't change anything. It'd only cause more pain, and there'd already been more than enough of that.

"The captain will send a squad to round up as many as they can," Fargo told her. Amity nodded as she muttered a thank you through eyes that said it was all beyond saving. She was right, of course. Royce Cantwell wouldn't be much interested in a few dozen steers when he'd agreed to over a hundred. But Fargo knew he had no choice but to play out the only plan he had. He watched Amity wander off through the slain cattle, looking terribly hurt and lost. He turned and rode to where Captain Duncan and the lieutenant stood together as they supervised the cleanup.

"It worked! You did it, Fargo. A lot of men, women, and children are going to live out their lives because of you and they won't really know it," Phil Duncan said.

"They will in time, every last one of them. I'll see to it," Lieutenant Jones said. "Thanks to you, I'm not at the end of a Dakota lance."

"The girl's cattle, what's left of them . . ." Fargo began, but the captain cut him off.

"I'm ahead of you, friend. I've already sent a squad out," he said. "I know what's churning inside you, but you did the right thing."

"Then why do I feel like some kind of Judas?" Fargo asked and rode away. He had gone a few hundred yards when the tall, unmistakable beaver hat came toward him.

"I know now why General Davis send you, Fargo. You find way to turn death to life, massacre to winning. I get word to him in my way. Maybe we meet again someday. You good man, Fargo."

"Much obliged. I'll take any kind words I can get," Fargo said with a lot more truth than manners, and the scout rode on with a tip of his beaver hat.

There was a good piece of the day left, and Fargo welcomed being alone as he halted to watch the captain start to lead most of his troops and their few prisoners back to the fort. In proper military procedure, they formed a column of twos, and he caught a flash of red hair amid the army blue and gold as the column disappeared across the flatland. He turned and rode on, stopping at a cluster of alders where a stream ran a few feet into the trees. He dismounted, then stretched out on the ground and wondered if time really healed all wounds or only those of the flesh. He catnapped as day wore into afternoon, when hoofbeats pounding hard awoke him. He sat up to see the horse and its rider, fiery red hair bouncing, as they raced toward him. A frown creased his brow as he saw Amity hold her horse at a gallop until she was but a foot away from him. He stepped back as she yanked the big bay to a halt and leaped from the saddle. He took a step toward her when her arm came up, her hand slapping him hard across the face.

"Bastard! Rotten, stinking bastard!" Amity screamed at him and, recovering from surprise, he managed to pull away from the nails that tried to rake his face. "Liar! Rotten, two-faced son-of-a-bitch liar!" she cursed at him, and he felt the pain of the kick that landed on his knee. Arms punching, flailing, hands outstretched to tear at the flesh of his face, she was a screaming dervish made of fury, and in each curse he heard a sob. "I overheard some of the troopers. Nobody made a mistake. You planned it, all of what you did. Damn you to hell, Skye Fargo!" she spat at him.

"Listen to me . . ." he started.

"No, never, never, never!" she half sobbed, half screamed, and flew at him again. He ducked away from her blows. Two more wild swings missed him, but he swore in pain as her foot raked his calf.

"Dammit, let me talk to you," he shouted but she had gone berserk, her hurt and pain fueling her fury. He had to duck from another slash of her nails that just grazed his cheek. She was at the edge of hysteria, he realized, beyond listening to reasoned explanations, beyond believing in any words he had for her. He needed something more than words to reach her and, parrying another onslaught of blows, he brought his fist up beneath her flailing arms, sinking it gently into her abdomen. The breath left her and she went down on her hands and knees, staying there gasping for air. He scooped her up and flung her facedown across the Ovaro and climbed into the saddle behind her.

Pulling the bay with him, he put the pinto into a canter, holding her facedown on the saddle as he rode. Her breath returned as they rode, and she flung angry accusations at him from facedown in the saddle. "You lied, betrayed me!" she shouted.

"That's right. I lied to you. I betrayed you," he agreed and he felt the surprise sweep through her, her accusations breaking off. "I had my reasons," he said.

"Yes, becoming a hero at my expense. Are you satisfied?" she threw back, and tried to push herself up, but he pressed her back down.

"Didn't do it for that," he said.

"Hell you didn't," she returned.

"Shut up, Amity Baker, just shut up!" he snapped.

"No, I won't. You can go to hell with your reasons. You're nothing but a liar, a false friend," she shot back.

He didn't answer, just kept his hand pressing her

down across the saddle as he reached the fort. Only when he rode into the compound still filled with settlers and their wagons, did he lift his hand as he halted. Dismounting, he pulled her roughly down from the Ovaro, tightly gripping her arm at the elbow. "This way," he growled.

"You're hurting me," she protested.

"Tough," he bit out as he pulled her along the first row of wagons. He paused at each one where little towheaded children waved back happily, their young faces beaming with beguiling innocence. He also stopped wherever six- or ten-year-olds smiled at them with trusting, young faces. He held Amity tightly, making her stop with him at each wagon and when he finished the first row, he pulled her down the second. When he passed the last wagon, he turned her around to face him. "You just saw my reasons, all those young lives that were doomed, to say nothing of the others. There was only one choice. It was your cattle or their lives, *all* of their lives. If you had to make that choice, you tell me what you'd have done. Go ahead, goddammit, tell me!" he said, his voice an abrasive snarl.

She glowered back at him but he saw in her round, pain-filled eyes a grudging, unspoken admission taking form. She swallowed hard, and he saw resentment replacing fury. "You should have told me," she said sullenly.

"Tell me you'd have agreed," he threw back at her and she didn't answer. "You wouldn't have," he answered for her, and realized a note of self-righteousness came into his voice. "You'd have argued, demanded I find another way, insisted I didn't need to use the cattle. You know it, Amity Baker. You wouldn't have agreed and there wasn't time for arguing and there wasn't another way and that's the whole of it."

He took her by the elbow again and marched her to where the Cleveland Bay waited beside the Ovaro. "Go your way, Amity Baker. Ride off and take your damn temper and anger with you. I don't care about either one anymore," he told her, swinging onto the pinto and riding away from her. He felt her glare following him as he rode from the fort. He set a slow pace as he headed along a line of aspen, the day now beginning to drift to an end. It was already dusk when he halted, sliding from the saddle beside a small arbor where grapes hung low from a thick bush. He set out his bedroll, and was starting to pull off his clothes when the sound of hooves came to him. He was waiting, hand on the Colt, when the rider emerged out of the night and he immediately recognized the Cleveland Bay by its bulk. He was standing as Amity dismounted and strode up to him, her manner curt.

"Captain Duncan's squad brought back twenty steers. Not much to show for all the years of work," she said. Fargo remained silent. "But I'm going to take them to Royce Cantwell. He can have a present of them if he wants," she added bitterly.

"Why'd you come telling me?" he asked.

"You made an agreement, and I'm still holding you to it," she said.

He considered for a moment. "Fair enough," he answered.

"Damn you, Fargo," Amity burst out and rushed forward, her lips pressing hard against his, her arms encircling his neck. "I hate you, I hate you," she murmured as she pulled his hand to her breasts and in moments she was naked atop him on the bedroll. All the fierce passion she had shown him previously now returned, only more so, a frenzied fury to her love-making. She screamed as she plunged herself onto his waiting erectness, breasts bouncing as she rode atop him, carrot red hair flying wildly. "Oh, God, oh God . . . aaaiiiieeee!" she screamed, a creature possessed, enveloped in berserk ecstasy. Her thighs rubbed against him as she continued her violent thrashing. She fell forward, pushing her milky white breasts into his mouth. "Hold me, hold me," she insisted, gasping out cries of pleasure until, with a suddenness that swept all else away, she exploded into quivering spasms. He came with her, unable to hold back as her passion caught everything up in its totality. Her back arched, breasts pointing upward, the tiny pink tips quivering. She clung to every moment, immersed in all-consuming pleasure and when the ecstasy spiraled away as it always did, her cry of protest echoed through the forest and shook the aspen's delicate leaves.

She fell atop him and lay still, soft murmurs coming from her lips. It was only when she pushed upward, her breasts swaying together, that he spoke. "You've a strange way of hating," he commented.

Her eyes speared into him. "Can you hate some-body and love them at the same time?" she mur-mured.

"Not usually, but I'll bet *you* can," he answered and she held on tightly to him, settling herself into the crook of his arm.

"The cattle are being held outside the fort," she said. "We'll pick them up in the morning."

"Are your hands with them?" he asked.

She shook her head. "The arrows got two of them in the midst of the attack, and the rest hightailed it out of there."

"The two of us should be able to herd twenty steers," Fargo said and she nodded agreement before going to sleep against him. When morning came, they breakfasted on the ripe grapes and she clung to him for a long moment before they began their ride to the fort. The night stayed with him as they rode, as good an example of the mysterious ways of women as he had ever come upon. Or, he had to ask himself, had it been only the ways of Amity Baker, with her flaming hair and a flaming temper? He'd not be trying to find out, he told himself. A pair of troopers with the cattle approached them as they reached the fort.

"The captain left orders for us to accompany you, miss," the one said, and Fargo nodded at Amity.

"Thank you," she replied, and the troopers fell in on both sides of the twenty steers as Fargo led the way on. He turned west, riding until the sun was high in the noon sky, then he swung the herd above the line of the river. He left her with the two troopers and rode ahead, and had gone perhaps another three miles when he reined to a halt. He drew in a deep breath and his lips tightened as the odor drifted to him, dark, dank, pungent. He rode slowly forward, the smell growing stronger and more pungent, and soon came into sight of a bog, wide and long, its very special, distinctive odor a part of the very air around it. He halted to take in the sheer size of the bog, and saw a man driving an Owensboro farm wagon skirting the edge of the bog.

He waited, and hailed the driver of the wagon as the man drew closer. "Looking for Royce Cantwell's place," he said, all but certain of the answer he'd get.

"Other side of the bog," the man replied, and Fargo swore under his breath.

"How long is it around?" Fargo asked.

"Five miles. Shortest way is through it. Cantwell's men do it all the time. There's a way through," the man said, pointing it out.

"Much obliged," Fargo said and the man drove on. Fargo's eyes returned to the bog and in the strange ways of memory, the odor took on form and meaning, all the times he'd smelled it returning to him. It was a sphagnum bog, home to the pitcher plant, rich peat moss, and all sorts of decaying matter that gave it that particular odor. Turning, he rode back to the herd. Amity had one more hurt in store for her. He couldn't prevent it, but maybe he could stop it from becoming something worse. When he reached her, he swung beside here, seeing the two troopers waiting on each side of the cattle. "There's a bog up ahead. When you reach it, go around it. I'll be going on ahead to Cantwell's place," he told her.

"Why?" she questioned.

"Want to check out the last part of the trail," he said. She accepted the answer but he saw a wariness come into her eyes, and he turned and rode quickly away.

When he returned to the bog he slowly nosed the horse to the edge and quickly spotted the strip of firm ground that cut through the center of the bog, just wide enough for a horse and rider to proceed single file. He steered the Ovaro onto the strip and started across the bog, its dark, pungent aroma assaulting him at once, clinging and cloying to all who passed through it. Long lines of pitcher plants grew on both sides of the narrow trail, their dark green-purple foliage a trap for every insect who alighted upon them. It was perhaps fitting that they grew here in front of Royce Cantwell's spread, deadly deceit their specialty, too. The strip of firm ground cut straight through the acrid ground and when Fargo reached the end of the bog he saw Cantwell's house and corrals a few thousand feet on. He rode from the narrow trail onto firm ground, and as he approached the house he saw a dozen or so Herefords in the corrals, a half-dozen ranch hands busy doing their chores, and a long bunkhouse off to the right. He paused at the bunkhouse, dismounted, and went inside, where an older man looked up from his bunk. "Royce Cantwell?" Fargo asked, as his eyes scanned the bunks in the long room.

"He'd be at the main house," the man answered, annoyance in his tone.

"Obliged," Fargo said and turned away. But he had seen what he wanted to see. There were sixteen bunks and ten of them were empty, all their personal gear and extra saddles gone. Fargo walked the few dozen yards to the main house, a well-built log structure with no particular character or impressiveness to it. He shot a glance at the hands, and saw that they had all moved in closer to the house. The door opened at his knock and a tall man in trousers and a checked shirt, a big Remington in his holster, stared back at him. "Royce Cantwell?" Fargo asked. The man nodded and Fargo took in his black hair and a face younger than he'd expected a see. He had a straight nose and brown eyes, a kind of hard handsomeness to the man.

"Who's asking?" Cantwell answered.

"Fargo, Skye Fargo. You don't know about me but I know about you."

"What do you know about me?" Cantwell challenged and Fargo saw his hand move to rest on his gun.

"I know that you're a murdering no-good bastard who tried to rustle Amity Baker's herd," Fargo said almost blandly.

Royce Cantwell's eyes narrowed. "Now how do you know that?" he asked. He grinned, but could not take the nervousness out of the smile.

"Let's say there's a certain smell about you and the

men you sent, the ones that were in those empty bunks," Fargo said.

The smile vanished from Royce Cantwell's face. "Seems you know a lot more than you should, mister," he said, his voice growing hard.

"If you're figuring to have your boys throw lead at me you ought to know that you'll be taking the first bullet," Fargo said almost blandly.

"My hand's on my gun and you figure to outdraw me?" Cantwell scoffed, but Fargo saw uncertainty touch the man's face.

"Count on it," Fargo said pleasantly. Cantwell didn't answer, the skepticism that had speared into him now changing to alarm.

"You could be bluffing, mister," Cantwell said.

"It's your call," Fargo said calmly and again Cantwell didn't answer. "I'd say we have us a Mexican standoff here," Fargo said. "Why don't we go inside and talk? There's still a way out of this for you."

The man nodded, and gestured for Fargo to follow him into the house. He wasn't being cooperative, Fargo knew. He was just waiting for a better chance to use his Remington, unwilling to risk drawing against so confident an opponent. Inside the living room, Fargo took in a modestly furnished house, most of it plain and very ordinary. "I'm listening," Royce Cantwell said.

"You made a deal with Amity, agreed to a price. You're going to pay it," Fargo said. He studied the man's sullen expression. "Why'd you do it, try to steal the herd?" Fargo asked. "Don't waste time denying it."

"You've no witnesses, nobody to pin it on me," Cantwell said.

"I've a nose. I don't need more than that," Fargo said. "Now why?"

"Lost most of my money in a dice game." Cantwell sighed.

"You'd nothing left to pay her when she delivered the herd?" Fargo said. The man's silence was an admission. Fargo cursed silently, his thought of making the man pay for his attempt at murder and rustling now blown away. If Cantwell could be believed, that is.

"Good story, not that I'm swallowing it. I'm thinking you just decided to get the herd for free before she reached you," Fargo said.

"I don't give a shit what you're thinking, mister, you're not walking out of here alive," Cantwell said with a snarl. Fargo's hand tensed as he thought Cantwell was about to draw, but the man kept hold of his fury, fear and caution stopping him from reaching for the Remington. Instead, he turned to a lamp on a table behind him, and began to light it. "I like plenty of light when I shoot somebody," he said and raised the lamp in the air. Fargo cursed as the sound of glass shattering filled the room, the two windows behind him showering glass onto the floor as a hail of bullets crashed through each. What he'd thought were caution and fear on Cantwell's part had been a signal, obviously long practiced.

Fargo dived, and rolled across the glass-strewn floor as shots hit the floorboards inches from him. He glimpsed Cantwell, Remington in hand, firing at him and felt the bullets graze his arm, then saw the six figures burst into the room through the door. Rolling into the hallway, Fargo avoided a volley of shots, which were fired furiously but wildly. From his prone position in the hallway, Fargo's marksmanship came to his rescue as he fired off three steady, controlled shots as three of the figures in the room collapsed in unison. Seeing another doorway from the hall, he rose and ran toward it just as another two of Cantwell's men ran into the hall. Fargo fired twice and the two men slammed backward into the wall of the narrow hallway, and slowly slid to the floor, leaving a red trail against the faded wallpaper of the corridor.

Dropping to one knee, Fargo was positioned and ready when the sixth man laid down a barrage as he ran into the hall. All the shots went harmlessly over his head as Fargo returned a single shot. The man spun, showering blood as he did until he pitched forward to the floor. Fargo stayed for a moment. Cantwell was somewhere, waiting for his chance. Fargo rose slowly, straining his ears for the sound of a door opening, or footsteps creeping across the floor or up a stairway. He was still listening, his brow furrowed, when he heard the sound of hoofbeats from outside. "Dammit," he swore. The man had run when the first barrage failed, and had raced from the house and now fled the scene on horseback. Whirling, Fargo bolted from the house, only to see that Cantwell had already disappeared from sight. He was just vaulting onto the Ovaro when a shot rang out from around the end of a line of cedars. Another shot followed instantly and Fargo sent the horse around the cedars, pulling to a halt at once. He saw Amity on the Cleveland Bay, a smoking rifle in her hands. She was alone, the cattle still somewhere behind her. His eyes went to the ground where Royce Cantwell's body lay facedown. Amity's eyes met his. "He pulled his Remington out to shoot me," she said. "He made it easy for me. I was on my way to return the favor. I smelled the odor from the bog and knew what it meant, just as you did. You didn't have to go on ahead."

"Thought maybe I could turn it all around for you. It didn't work out," he replied.

"You tried," she said.

"What are you going to do now?" he asked.

"I told you I've a few calves left at home. I'll take the twenty left here back with me. I'll start all over. Maybe I'll have better luck next time," she said, pausing, her eyes reaching deep into his. "I'll expect you'll take me back," she said with an edge of tartness.

"Sort of thought you'd stopped being mad at me. Or did I dream last night?" Fargo said.

"You had a powerfully good reason for what you did, but it still did me wrong. I still think that needs paying back," she said.

"You've something in mind?" he asked.

"I figure making love to me every night till we get back and then more," she said, moving the bay forward, leaning over in the saddle, her lips warm and wet on his. "Deal?" she murmured.

"Deal," he said, turning the pinto and rode at her side. Flaming red hair and flaming passion was a kind of punishment he'd welcome. And from now on, he'd be sure to do the right thing for the right reason, he promised himself.

LOOKING FORWARD!
The following is the opening
section from the next novel in the exciting
Trailsman series from Signet:

THE TRAILSMAN #213
APACHE WELLS

New Mexico, 1860—
where red men and white men clashed
in a battle no one could win . . .

Fort Breckinridge was new to San Pedro, New Mexico. For years, the area had depended solely on Fort Buchanan as its defense against the Apache. However, due largely to the overland mail route traveled by John Butterfield's stage line between St. Louis and San Francisco, Fort Breckinridge had to be built. The stage line crossed the paths of many Indian raiding trails. In fact, west of El Paso there was no protection at all, until Fort Breckinridge was erected.

Skye Fargo rode toward the fort, knowing that he would find what he found at every such outpost. He had, however, promised his friend, John Butterfield, that he would take a look at the new fort and send him a telegram describing what he found.

Two years earlier, Fargo had helped Butterfield map out his route from St. Louis to San Francisco. It was for this reason that Fargo felt he still had an obligation to the man—an obligation that went beyond friendship.

The Apaches in this area were supposed to be peaceful—or, at least, that's what he had been told in 1859 by the Indian agent, Michael Steck. Fargo took Steck at his word, finished mapping out the route, and then returned to St. Louis to show it to Butterfield.

During the course of the last two years, many of Butterfield's coaches had been hit by Apaches. Fargo, though not connected with Butterfield's company, nevertheless felt responsible. It was while he was in St. Louis recently that Butterfield came to him about Fort Breckinridge. . . .

"After all this time," Butterfield said, "I'm thinking of changing the route ya mapped out."

"I don't blame you," Fargo said. "Have a new one mapped out by someone you trust, this time."

"I trust you," Butterfield said.

They were in a tavern near the river and the men around them were mostly dockworkers. Butterfield professed to prefer their company to any other when it came to drinking.

"You mean you trusted me," Fargo said, "and look what happened."

"I can't hold ya responsible for what a bunch of redskins do, Fargo," Butterfield said. He brushed foam from his huge mustache with the back of his hand, first one side, then the other.

"What would you like me to do, Jim?"

"I'd like ya to go and take a look at this fort," Butterfield said. "Tell me if it's gonna make a difference or not—and if not, then find me another route."

Fargo played with his beer mug, making wet circles with it on the bottom on the table.

"I'll pay ya."

"No, you won't," Fargo said. "If I do this, I'll just be finishing the job I started two years ago."

"Ah!" Butterfield said, waving a hand. "That job is done and paid for. This is a new one, and I'll pay ya for it. No argument."

"If I take it."

"You'll take it."

Fargo grinned.

"Why do you say that?"

"Because I know ya," Butterfield said. "I know you feel responsible for what's happened these past two years—ya shouldn't, but I know ya do."

"And you'll take advantage of that?"

"If I was gonna take advantage of ya," Butterfield said, "would I be insistin' on payin' ya?"

"All right," Fargo said, "I'll go and take a look."

"If this fort will do the trick and police that area well enough," Butterfield said, "this won't be a long job for ya."

"But if it isn't going to do the job and keep Cochise

and the others in line," Fargo said, "it will be a very long job."

"And I'll pay ya well for every bit of it," Butterfield said. "Is it a deal?"

He stuck out his hand.

Fargo accepted it.

"All right," he said resignedly, "it's a deal . . ."

He could see the fort long before he reached it. It had been built right near the San Pedro River and wasn't all that far from Fort Buchanan. Fargo really didn't understand the placement of this new fort. If they really wanted to fortify the area, it should have been built further away from its sister fort, so that between them they could cover more ground.

That was the first mistake he was going to have to inform John Butterfield of.

However, even before riding to Fort Breckinridge, Fargo had to first stop at the Butterfield stage station at Apache Wells.

As Fargo rode up to the station, the door of the small stone building opened and a man stepped out, holding a rifle. When he saw who it was, he immediately dropped the barrel of the rifle toward the ground, but he did not put the weapon down.

"Skye Fargo, as I live and breathe," he said, as Fargo reigned in the Ovaro and dismounted. "How long's it been?"

Fargo extended his hand to the man and said, "How long you been out here, Andy?"

"Nigh on to two years."

"Well then, that's how long it's been. You got anything wet inside?"

"Nothin' cold," Andy Culhane said, "but I got coffee, and a jug to sweeten it with."

"Let's get to it, then."

Fargo tied off the Ovaro and the two men went inside. Only when the door was closed and bolted did Culhane put the rifle down. He spotted Fargo watching him while he did it and shook his head.

"Things ain't good around here, Fargo," he said. "Ain't good at all."

"I thought you got along with the Indians now," Fargo said. "At least, that's what Butterfield told me."

"I do," Culhane said, retrieving two cups and a pot of coffee from the stove. "I have no problem with the Coyoteros and the Chiricahuas, but the Pinals . . . they'd just as soon shoot me as look at me."

"What'd you do to them?"

Culhane poured two cups of coffee, carried the black pot back to the stove, then returned carrying a jug of whiskey. He sat, uncorked the jug, and spiked both cups of coffee with the potent liquor inside.

"It ain't me," he said, "it's anybody."

"I thought this was supposed to be under control two years ago?"

"It was supposed to be," Culhane said, "but it ain't. Salute."

They clinked cups and drank some coffee. Fargo felt it slide down his throat, cutting the trail dust as it went. When it reached his belly, it started a little fire there.

"What brings you out there again, Skye?" Culhane asked.

"Butterfield asked me to look into this new fort," Fargo said.

"Breckinridge," Culhane said, nodding. "Damn fools built the thing too close to Fort Buchanan, you ask me."

"I noticed that myself."

"Ain't gonna do nobody much good where it is," Culhane said. "What's Butterfield want you to do?"

"Take a look at the fort and see if he needs a new route or not."

"And if he does?"

"Then I'm to map it out."

"You come talk to me if you've a mind to," Culhane said. "I got some ideas."

"I'll do that," Fargo said. He finished the coffee and set the cup down.

"More?" Culhane asked.

"No, that'll hold me."

"How 'bout without the coffee to dilute it?" the station manager asked with a smile.

"I don't think so, Andy," Fargo said. "I don't want to fall off my horse between here and the fort."

"Be a touch of Apaches there to help you up if you do," Culhane said, "and to help themselves to what's yours."

"I'll keep that in mind."

Both men walked to the door and Culhane picked up his rifle before he unbolted it.

"I'll water my horse before I leave," Fargo said.

"Help yourself to the well. I'll keep watch."

Fargo walked the Ovaro to the well, sank the bucket, and cranked it back up. He had a bit himself—it was cold, and refreshing after the coffee—then he held the bucket while the horse had his fill. That done, he set the bucket aside, mounted up, waved to Culhane, and rode off toward Fort Breckinridge.